Black Authors INK Presents

Gotta $\mathcal{B}$more Careful

A Novel by
Tammy Hawk

Gotta *B*more Careful
Copyright © 2017 Tammy Hawk

For information regarding special discounts for wholesale purchases, please contact Black Authors Ink Sales at blackauthorsink@gmail.com or mail inquiry to Black Authors Ink Llc, P.O. Box 271, Mauldin, SC 29662

ISBN-10:0997157240
ISBN-13: 978-0997157246

Editor: Olivia Shaw
Cover Design: Jesse Burrell
Formatting: Shenaka Sullivan

First Black Authors Ink Trade Paperback Edition 2017
Printed in the United States of America

Black Authors Ink LLC
P.O. Box 271
Mauldin, SC 29662

DEDICATION

Dedicated to the memory of

James E. Sanders, Sr.

May you forever remain in our hearts.

Thank you for your faith and support.

We love you, Pops.

"Keep your head up and represent"

ACKNOWLEDGEMENTS

First, I would like to give all glory to God, for without Him, none of this would be possible. To my two wonderful children Sariah and Jason Jr., you guys have brought nothing but joy into my life and I thank the both of you for loving me unconditionally. You are my world and mommy loves you dearly.

Jonathan Sanders: I appreciate your patience, love, and understanding. I know I'm not always the easiest person to deal with but you take my sharp words and stubbornness like a champ.

Mom, what can I say? You are truly my rock and you have always been there for me through thick and thin, the good and the bad. I love you so much. To my siblings Blandine Reid, DeWayne Hawk, and Tameka Brown: I love you guys and miss you all like crazy.

Rick Parham, you stepped up and became a father figure and a wonderful grandpa, I can never thank you enough. You didn't have to do it, but you did.

Ms. Shenaka Sullivan, you noticed my talent and encouraged me through this endeavor. Thank you for your mentorship and guidance. I hope I made you proud.

Last but certainly not least THANK YOU, THANK YOU, THANK YOU to ALL of my friends and family in the great states of Maryland and Louisiana for your support. The book you all have been waiting for has finally arrived. I hope you enjoy it and look forward to the next one. I have many more stories to tell; this is just the tip of the iceberg. Without further ado, I present to you, Gotta Bmore Careful.

-Tammy Hawk

"If Stephen King can do it, why can't I?"

Tammy Hawk

CHAPTER 1

I never thought I'd be here, stuck in Louisiana, facing jail time behind some bullshit. My momma told me this place would be my downfall. Honestly, I can't blame anyone or anything for what I've done. I got these demons, I can't control myself. Lord have mercy...

TOYA

One year ago...

"Hey, bae. You packed and ready to come see me?" Clyde swooned on the phone.

I'm smiling from ear to ear, happy that I am finally moving to Louisiana to be with my man.

"You there?" I can hear him pull the phone away from his ear, probably to look at the screen to see if the call disconnected.

"Yeah, I'm here. Just a little excited and nervous."

I'm not used to big bugs, a bunch of trees, or overly friendly country folk. Shit, I'm not used to the south, period! Baltimore has always been my home and leaving my city is bittersweet, but it's a sacrifice that I am willing to make for Clyde.

"Okay, bae. Well, I'll see ya soon and stop worrying. I got you," he says.

"Alright, I'll see you when I land. Love you," I tell him.

"Love ya too," he replied and hung up.

I look around my condo one last time, take a deep breath, and walk out the door.

"Bitch, I know you're not leaving!" I turn around to face my best friend Sonya.

"Bitch, I called you three times this morning," I say as I squint my eyes and poke her in the chest.

"My bad, girl. Shit, Marques was eating this kitty like it was his last meal," she says as she does a freaky little dance.

"You're such a skank." I laugh.

"But on a serious note, Imma miss the hell outta you." She frowned.

"Give me one year to settle in and get my ducks in a row. Then I can get you down there and we can get shit poppin'." I wink at her.

"I hope those country muthafuckas are ready for what we're bringing," Sonya says and looks at me with mischief in her eyes.

All I can do is nod and hug her. In the back of my mind, I'm wondering the same thing. I'm not just going to Louisiana to be with Clyde, but to expand my business as well, because at the end of the day, it's money over everything. I'm about my paper first and that will never change, not even for love.

***

Sonya

Damn, I hate to see my girl leave but it's to benefit us. I sit on the edge of my bed and stare at a picture of Toya and I. We've been thick as thieves since the third grade. I smile, reminiscing about the first time we met. I had just moved to Baltimore from D.C. and got beat up on my first day of school. As soon as I walked into the classroom, all eyes were on me. The boys smiled but the girls snickered and rolled their eyes. To put icing on the cake, the teacher made me introduce myself to the class and told them that I was from D.C. That put a bullseye on my ass from that point on, but one girl stood out to me. Not once did she look in my direction. She just stared out the window, tapping her pencil on her desk.

During lunch I sat alone because the other kids refused to let me sit next to them, which I didn't care; I'm a loner anyway. I couldn't help but stare at that quiet little girl as I chewed on my cold fries and odd colored hot dog. She was very pretty. Her hair was long, light brown, and had big curls. The other kids sat around her and talked to her or played in her hair but she seemed uninterested. She just nodded once in a while to whatever they were saying. She was obviously pretty popular despite her clothes being dingy. Something about her intrigued me but I couldn't figure out why.

When recess finally came around, the moment I was dreading happened. I was minding my own business, jump roping. Occasionally, I would glance at the mystery girl sitting on the bench surrounded by her friends. She didn't talk much. All of a sudden I felt a strong push come from behind me and I fell to the ground. I looked up and saw this big, ugly thing looking down at me with her arms crossed over her stomach. I say thing, because this big, burly bitch looked like Magilla Gorilla.

"Watch where you goin'," she snarled. Her two friends stood next to her laughing at my expense.

"Don't you know y'all D.C. bitches ain't welcome in Bmore?" Congo's friend squealed. She was tall, thin and had bug eyes. All I could do was laugh, which was a big mistake because it pissed them off. Next thing I knew, I could feel hands and shoes making contact with my body. That beat down didn't last long because mystery girl got off the bench and approached us with two of her friends.

Next thing I know, mystery girl's fist makes contact with Mighty Joe Young's face. That must have been the signal for her two friends to commence to whooping the gorilla's two friends' asses. Something about mystery girl's eyes scared me. It was like something evil came over her as she pummeled the fat girl's face. All I could think was, what the fuck? Eventually, the teachers were able to break up the brawl and send us all to the principal's office. As we sat outside of the office, I contemplated on speaking to the mystery girl but felt that the moment was not right.

"You aight?" she asked.

I look to my right and see these beautiful chestnut brown eyes staring me in my face. I'm not a lesbian, but she was gorgeous. Her smooth skin was the color of golden honey, and her hair was long and silky but unkept. Her clothes were drabby, but she was still beautiful. I could see why the other kids flocked to her. She had a strong presence.

"Hellooo…" She snapped her fingers in my face.

"Huh? Oh! Yeah, I'm good. Thanks for what you did back there," I said.

"Don't worry about it. I just can't stand bullies," she replied.

Again that deadly look resurfaced on her face and I swear when the light hit her eyes, them bitches looked red.

"What's your name?" I asked.

Just as fast as that look had reappeared, it went away. She smiled. "I'm Toya. What's yours?"

"Sonya. I told y'all that in class this morning when I first came in," I said.

"Oh! Well, I must not have heard you. Anyway, nice to meet you Sonya."

From that moment on, we became best friends.

"Sonya!" Marques stood in front of me clearly irritated.

"What, boy?" I shout as I watch him pull his shirt over his dark chocolate chiseled frame.

"I said I'm about to head out. I gotta make some dough," he repeats.

"Aight, boo. Go on and get your paper. I'm thinking about hitting up White Marsh Mall today," I say as I grab my Gucci bag and shades.

"Take the Honda so you can be low-key. You know these pigs will pull you over if you take the Benz." I smirk. He grabs the keys off the dresser, kisses my forehead, and heads out the door. I pick up my phone and dial contact number two.

"What's good, beautiful?" Trey says into the phone.

"I'm on my way to pick up that money. I got some shopping to do," I speak in code. "Say no more, I got dat," he says and hangs up.

CHAPTER 2

Clyde

After getting off the phone with Toya, I went to my closet to put an outfit together for the special day. I opted for my black True Religion jeans, a red, black and white button down True Religion shirt, and my red Retro Jordans.

BANG! BANG! BANG!

"Da fuck bangin' on my door like dat? Who is it?" I shout.

"Open the door, bruh!" Mookie yelled.

I open the door and look at the stupid expression on this fool's face. "You just gone stand there lookin' dumb or come in?" I ask.

"What I tell you 'bout answerin' the door in yo boxers, nigga?" Mookie capped back.

"I told you I gotta get my gul from da airport. Shit, I'm bout to take a shower, get dressed, and head on out," I explain.

"I can ride wit you?" he asks.

"Hell naw! My gul ain't ready ta meet nobody. She a city gul and not too keen on new faces," I explain.

"Fuck it den. Roll one up," he says.

"Here nigga, take dis gram and leave. I got shit to do, bruh." I toss Mookie a sac and head towards my bathroom. "You can let yourself out," I yell from the bathroom. As I step into my shower, I can hear my door slam.

Mookie is my nigga, but he stay bumming. That muthafucka always want something. I had already put him up on game, fronted him some loud to make some bread, and hooked him up with my sister. What more could I do? I made sure he was straight as soon as he got out of jail but he always wants more. I think it's about time he and I have a serious talk soon.

After taking my shower and getting dressed, I take one last look in the mirror. I must admit, I'm a fly ass nigga. I have milk chocolate skin, standing at six foot three, with a clean fade. I have straight, snow white teeth, with golds on my K9s, and a perfect goatee. I stay dressed fresh; these hoes be jockin' on a nigga. I laugh to myself as I grab my keys and head out the door. Yeah, I know I'm cocky, but it's true. I stay getting pussy on a daily. Now that Toya is coming down here, Imma have to be careful with these thots. What she doesn't know won't hurt her. Right?

***

Toya

As I'm putting my carry-on bag in the overhead compartment, some white boy has the audacity to walk into me and knock me over. To add insult to injury, the bitch ass cracker didn't help me up, but it's cool. I get up and dust myself off, taking my seat. After the plane ascends into the air, I begin to look around to see where that cracker is sitting. Instinctively I begin playing with the cross on my chain.

There he is, sitting behind the girl across from me. We make eye contact and at that moment I know that I got his full attention. I was always told that I have bedroom eyes, so I use them to my advantage. I wink, bite my bottom lip, and look him up and down. He looks towards the bathroom and back at me. I got him! I nod and sashay towards the bathroom.

Carefully making sure to open the door with my shirt, I enter, sit on the sink, and wait. About five minutes later, he enters and locks the door. I grab him by the collar of his shirt and pull him towards me. As I'm sticking my tongue down his throat and unbuckling his belt, I can hear him opening a condom wrapper.

"You ready to help me join the mile high club?" I whisper in his ear.

Without any words he turns me around and bends me over.

"Nuh, playboy. My pussy, my rules," I say as I turn back around and push him onto the toilet. "Take my panties off," I demand.

He obliges, slowly removing my thong.

"Now put them in your mouth," I say seductively.

"What…" He tries to protest but I quickly grab my panties out of his hand, stuff them in his mouth, and straddle him.

"Good boy." I smile and pat him on the head. I stand up and let him put his condom on, as I lick and nibble on his ear. He was so into it that he didn't notice me yank the chain off my neck.

"I'm gonna fuck the shit outta you," I say as I slowly sit on his stiff little peanut of a dick.

I'm riding him nice and slow, moaning, and rolling my eyes in the back of my head. *I should get an Oscar from my acting skills*, I think in the back of my head. By the look on his face, I can tell that he cannot handle my phat, juicy peach. I take off my shirt and toss it towards the sink; he's moaning. He puts his head back and closes his eyes.

Gripping my cross in my hand, I make one swift move across his neck, from ear to ear. I place my hand over his mouth, making sure that my panties do not fall out. He's bucking and bleeding out. I cum all over his lil' dick; all that bucking brings me to an orgasm. Fuck! That was good! I get up, remove my panties from his mouth, and put them back on.

"Make sure you clean up," I say to myself. I rinse off in the sink and grab the condom off his dick. I realize that I literally fucked the shit outta him; this fool released his bowels. I flush it and use the shirt that I had took off to wipe down any and everything I touched.

"Watch where the fuck you goin' next time," I say as I exit out the bathroom. Sitting back in my seat, I smile at the thought of seeing Clyde. Next stop: Louisiana!

"Ready or not, here I come." I laugh to myself.

CHAPTER 3

Sonya

On the way to meet up with Trey, I look at all of the boarded up row houses and shake my head. Suddenly I slam on my brakes, put my car in park, and get out. "Whose baby is this in the middle of the muthafucking street?" I shout toward a group of niggas on the corner.

I see a dread head slowly approach me with a look on his face like he wants to fight me. I take off my Gucci shades, put my hands on my hips, and tilt my head to the side. I hope this fool doesn't think I'm scared. Instinctively I feel for my Beretta tucked behind me and switch the safety off.

"Bitch, don't come up here on our corner causing a scene. Drive around the lil' nigga." He smirked.

"Oh, so you think you funny huh?" I laugh.

"Yeah, bitch. As a matter of fact, I do. What'll be funnier is this dick in ya mouth." He grabbed his crotch.

I guess that was my cue to boost his ego, so I approach him slowly. I place my right hand on his chest and my lips to his ear. "Put this dick in your mouth," I whisper. He looks down at the gun pressed against his crotch in shock. This bitch pissed on himself then put his hands up in surrender. I walk around him with my gun trained on him with a smirk on my face. I can hear a bunch of footsteps coming up behind me. CLICK. Someone cocks their gun.

"Aight, bitch. You had your fun. Let my nigga go," a deep voice comes from behind me. I know that voice from anywhere.

"Gutta, I suggest you tell your little thugs to step back right fuckin' now!" I grit my teeth.

He walks around to face me and all the color drains from his face. "Yo, y'all step back and put dem guns down," he says with authority.

"You need to teach your goons some respect, Gutta." I smile.

"Shit, that's my bad, Sonya. I didn't realize dat was you," his voice shook.

I stand next to Gutta and look the dread head up and down. "Get on your knees," I demand.

"What the fuck? Gutta, you gonna let this bi…" he tries to protest.

I cut him off with the butt of my gun, breaking the bridge of his nose. He grabs his face with wide eyes and shook.

"Do what she says, Los," Gutta instructs.

Los gets on his knees and looks up at me with a quizzical look on his face.

"Gutta, how about you explain to Los and the rest of these peons who the fuck I am so that we don't have this misunderstanding again," I say as I put the safety back on my Beretta.

"Y'all, this is Toya's right hand. She is to be respected—no exceptions," he explains.

"Yo, Gutta, I ain't know," Los tries to explain.

I place my fingers to his lips. "Ssshhh. No hard feelings. You didn't know, so I give you my word that I won't kill you." I smile.

Los sighs in relief, grateful that his life was spared.

"You little muthafuckas need to come over here and clean up this mess," I say.

They looked at me confused.

"Gutta," I look at him.

"Yeah?" he responds.

"Kill 'em," I demand.

Without hesitation, Gutta takes out his forty-five and relieves Los of his miserable life. I bust out laughing at the look on everyones face.

"I gave him my word that I wouldn't kill him. Be glad it was me that he disrespected and not Toya," I say with a serious look on my face. "Well? What the fuck y'all waiting for? Clean this trash up and take that damn baby home," I yell.

I look at Gutta, smile, and put my shades back on. He nods at me as I get back in my Benz and pull off. When are these niggas gonna ever learn?

***

Marques

If there's one thing I can't stand, it's a bitch that calls over and over again if I don't answer my phone. Looking at my phone, I see twelve missed calls from the same damn number. I turn the ringer on and call the number back.

"Who's this?" Keisha screams into the phone.

"Bitch, you know who it is. Stop playing," I cap at her.

"Nigga, I called you five hundred times and you didn't answer the phone! What if it was an emergency? You so…" she continues so I put the phone in my lap and make another call on my second phone.

"You have reached the voicemail of four four three…"

"Hey baby, I was just calling to see if you want to go out to eat tonight. Hit me back," I leave a message and hang up. Taking a deep breath, I pick the phone up from my lap.

"Hello?" Keisha yells into the phone.

"Yeah," I reply.

"I know you ain't just call a whole 'nother bitch while I'm on the phone wit'chu." She was irate.

I hold in my laugh 'cause this is just too damn funny. "Look, you called me twelve times. The fuck you want, Keisha?" I sigh. I swear this hoe is a headache, but the bitch is a certified freak, so I tolerate her little antics.

"I just wanted to see you, daddy," she whines.

"You miss daddy dick?" I ask.

"I need it, baby. I'm nice and wet for you," Keisha purrs.

"Aight, give me about two hours and I'll come through," I say and hang up. I reach into my glove box for my throw away and speed dial number one.

"What's good, yo?" I hear on the other end.

"I'm on my way," I say and hang up. I speed dial number two next.

"Hello?" a sexy voice comes over the phone.

"What's good, love?" I ask.

"Hey, baby, I'm ready," Ginger coos.

"Is everything ready?" I ask.

"Yeah, just waiting on you to give me a ride home," she replies.

"That's what's up. I'm on my way," I tell her and hang up.

Heading down East Baltimore, I spot Sonya. I wonder what she's doing over here. Once I get to the strip club, I park my car and get out. "Sup, Bull?" I ask as I approach the bouncer at the door.

"Shit, I can't call it ock," he replies and waves me in.

I spot Ginger at the bar talking to the bartender and continue to walk towards the bathroom.

"What's up, Marques?" the big cock diesel bouncer asks.

I give him a head nod as I enter the bathroom. I go into the second stall and lift up the back of the toilet to retrieve my three-eighty. "Good seeing you, Truck," I say to the bouncer as I exit the bathroom and slip him a bill.

As I walk towards the owner's office, I wink at Ginger and she continues to talk to the bartender as if she didn't see me. I look into the camera above the entrance to the office and the door buzzes open.

"Marques, what's up, my friend?" Ahmed approaches me and daps me up.

I sit on the red leather couch across from his desk and look at the security footage mounted on the wall. "How's business, Ahmed?" I ask.

He looks around everywhere but avoids eye contact with me.

"Open the door for Ginger."

I nod towards the security screen to let him know that she's standing outside the door. *BZZZ.* Ginger walks in with her pink rolling luggage and places it on Ahmed's desk. I open the luggage and remove the few garments that were placed in it. I look towards Ahmed and he quickly walks towards the red couch. Ahmed slides the couch over and opens a safe that he had built into the floor.

"About the money, Marques. It's a little short," Ahmed says nervously as he starts handing me stacks.

"How short, nigga?" I ask.

He stands up and dusts his pants off. "Um. About two hundred thousand," the short, fat fuck replies.

I don't even say anything to him. I just reach into my pocket.

"Hold on, Marques! It doesn't have to be like this! I can get you the money!" He falls to his knees, crying for mercy.

All I can do is shake my head in disgust. I pull out my phone and he breathes a sigh of relief. I scroll to my contact, Boss Lady.

"Hello?" she answers.

"Toya, this nigga Ahmed is a little confused," I reply.

"How confused?" she asks.

"Number two hundred on the exam," I answer.

"How many questions are there total?" she asks.

"Five hundred total," I tell her.

"Put him on the phone," Toya demands.

I hand the phone to Ahmed. I don't know what the fuck she said to him, but the nigga fainted.

CHAPTER 4

Clyde

As soon as I see Toya come through the gate, a smile spreads across her face. She walks over to me and hugs me around my neck. "How was your flight, bae?" I ask.

Her body becomes tense and she breaks her embrace. I've seen that look before; her eyes, I don't know how to explain it. She's smiling though.

"It was great, the ride was a little bumpy." She smirks.

When we arrive at baggage claim, her phone begins to ring. "Hello?...How confused?...How many questions are there total?..." Toya's face turns beet red. "Put him on the phone." She grits her teeth.

I grab her luggage and turn around to hear the rest of the conversation. "If you don't pass this exam, I'm going to have to call your wife. Your children would be so disappointed," she says with a devious smile. "Marques, I'm calling Sonya. Make sure you answer your phone when I call," she says into the phone.

I automatically know that somebody's family is in trouble. Toya starts tapping her foot, clearly irritated. "Sonya, Ahmed failed an exam. He can retake the test tomorrow to make up the points and if he fails to do so, please call his wife and make sure he's cut from the class. Thanks," Toya instructs and hangs up.

I try to put my arm around her to calm her down, but she wasn't having it.

"Not right now, Clyde." She pushes my arm away.

"Da fuck I do?" I ask.

"Nigga, I said NOT! RIGHT! NOW!" she yells and storms towards the exit.

Everyone in baggage claim watched her in shock as she walked out. I walk after her, shaking my head in embarrassment. *Damn, yellabone's crazy as hell,* I think to myself. The look on her face said it all. This crazy bitch was happy and mad at the same damn time. Lord have mercy on whoever pissed her off.

***

Toya

"Why is it that as soon as I leave Bmore, muthafuckas wanna act up? I mean, I'm not a bad person, at least I don't think I am. A lot of niggas are eating good back home, I make sure of that. Sonya will get it handled, so stop stressing. You need to focus on getting things set up in Louisiana. I know! I know! You got this Toya! You're right, I got this!"

"Bae!" Clyde yells in my face.

"Huh? What you say?" I ask.

"I said, what was dat back dere. Yeah?" he asks.

"Nothing I can't handle, boo. I apologize for going off on you," I say and kiss him passionately.

"You need ta learn how ta control yo anger," he huffs.

"I know, baby. I'll try my best to keep my temper in check," I pout.

The ride from New Orleans to Alexandria took three hours. The trip was pretty interesting. The causeway was a long stretch, over twenty-four miles long. What really threw me off was the music that was playing on the radio. "Why does the music sound like that?" I ask.

Clyde glances at me and smiles, "Dat's DJ Screw."

"I don't know if I wanna fall asleep or bob my head," I tell him.

Clyde busts out laughing as if I told a joke, but I was serious. When we arrive in Alexandria, I peeped the scenery. There were a lot of trees, boarded up vacant houses and shacks, and it was very quiet except for a few cars passing by with the trunks rattling from too much bass. It seems like a really low-key town. It's a complete culture shock to me, the total opposite of Baltimore.

"This will take some getting use to," I tell Clyde.

"You'll be fine, bae. Down here we ride slow." He smiles.

"Who's that waving at me? I don't know him!" I smirk.

"Get used to it. People are just more friendly down here," Clyde explains.

I wonder if people will still like me once I get things jumping down here. Overall, I like what I see. It won't be hard to get business started down here. "What's poppin' down here?" I ask Clyde.

"Shit, pain meds, Xanax, heroin, meth, coke, and weed," he replies.

I nod my head, calculating how much I was going to profit. The first thing I need to do is observe everything, and find out who will be my competition or cause problems, and make sure I eliminate them.

CHAPTER 5

Mookie

I've been trying to figure out how I can get into this house for the past three months. This nigga got cameras all around this bitch. The alarm system and reinforced locks make it even more impossible. I'm far from stupid though. I got a plan that I know will definitely work. It'll just take a little time and patience to rob this nigga blind. Clyde always thought he was better than me. Nigga thinks his shit don't stink. It's about time someone knocks him off his high horse. He's lucky he didn't let me ride to the airport with him. I sure was going to put my pistol to the back of his girl seat and make him drive back to A-Town. I would have made that nigga empty out that muthafuckin' safe, then kill him and his bitch.

I unclip my phone from my side to call him. "You on your way back, bo?" I ask as soon as he picks up.

"Damn, nigga. Why you keeping tabs on me? You worse den a bitch," Clyde barks into the phone.

"I gotta holla atchu bout somethin' bruh," I explain.

"Fuck, mane! Can a nigga get his guh settled in before you start beggin' me for shit?" he huffs into the phone.

"Why you trippin' bruh? I ain't say nothin' 'bout wantin' a muthafuckin' thang from yo ass. Ugh, nigga get yo head outcho ass, bruh," I cap back at him.

"Look, you better make this visit quick bruh, real talk. I ain't got time to entertain you. My guh is on one right nah and I ain't tryin' to hear her mouth over your dumb shit. I'm 'bout ten minutes away," Clyde says and hangs up.

I can't stand that nigga! I can't wait to kill his ass. I might just fuck his bitch in front of him before I kill both of them.

Forty-five minutes later, Clyde pulls up and exits the car. "Nigga, you said ten minutes," I complain.

"What you want bo?" he walks towards the trunk.

"Look, I got somebody dat's sellin' some flat screens for cheap in the Sonya Quarters," I say as I look into the car.

I see the finest bitch I've ever seen in my life. Yellabone with long, good hair. I can see that she is thick in all the right places and her smile is flawless. She's looking at me and waves then points down towards her lap. I look down and this bitch got Clyde's gun pointed at me. She rolls down her window, still smiling at me.

"If you don't get out my muthafuckin' face, Imma dead ya ass right fucking here," she says.

I quickly back up with both of my hands up. She waves goodbye to me, still smiling, and rolls up her window. Then has the nerve to wink at me and bite her bottom lip. I walk towards Clyde to help him carry her luggage.

"You got a good look at my guh?" he asks.

"She fine as hell, bo." I smile.

"Good, well let dat be da last time you stare all in her face. She off limits. Plus the only guh you need to be worryin' 'bout is my sista," Clyde threatens.

"Trust me, I won't. Ya guh just made dat very clear," I laugh.

"Laugh now, cry later," I hear from behind me. There she stands, staring at me with the look of death in her eyes. Right then and there, I knew that bitch was pure evil. I also realized that robbing and killing them would be a lot harder then I thought.

***

Sonya

When I finally reach Park Heights to meet up with Trey, my phone rings. "Hey girl! How was your trip? I miss you already," I answer.

Toya goes into a rant about how Ahmed was two hundred points short from passing an exam and that he had until tomorrow to make up the credits or his wife is to receive a house call. "I got you, no worries." I hang up and quickly call Marques. He answers the phone on the first ring. "What's the damage?" I ask.

"Five hundred points total, two hundred points short," he explains.

"You on East Baltimore, right?" I ask.

"Yeah. I'm not going anywhere," Marques responds. "Okay, look. I'm in Park Heights handling something. Give me about an hour or so." I hang up and exit my car.

Trey is on the stoop, talking to his boys, and tells them to clear out as I approach him. "What's up, ma? You ready to get this over with?" he asks.

"Ready as I'll ever be," I reply as we enter the house. I head towards the back window and see a long line of fiends getting served. "I see business is good. The blue tops are selling. How about the yellow caps?" I inquire.

"Yeah, those packages Beast and Sincere delivered are monsters," Trey says.

"Good, 'cause I got twenty more kilos for you. Expect Beast and Sincere to be here tomorrow," I tell him.

"Bet, I'll be here. Let's go get your package," Trey says and leads me upstairs.

I knock on a door that leads to one of the rooms and a metal plate slides open to some peering eyes. Shortly after the plate closes, the door unlocks from the inside. We enter into a room with five females dressed in nothing but panties.

"Corey, bring her the bag," Trey instructs the tar black guy sitting in the corner of the room with an A.K. He approaches me and hands me the duffle bag full of money.

"It's all there, boss," Corey says in his deep, baritone voice.

I begin to walk around the table that the females are working at; they continue to put cocaine in vials as if I wasn't there. I step closer to get a better look at the product. Nothing but fish scale sparkling up the table. I pick up a vial with a yellow cap and admire the powder inside. I nod my head in approval, put the vial down, and walk out the room followed by Trey. Corey closes and locks the door behind us.

I knock on a second door and once again, I am met with eyes peering at me from a slot in the door. The door unlocks from the inside and we walk into the second room. Once again, there are five females just like the previous room, except they were putting crack into vials with blue tops. In the corner of the room sat Dro with an AR15. He gives us a head nod and continues to watch the women work around the table. Satisfied with what I see, I exit the room and begin to walk downstairs.

"Hold up. Before you go downstairs." Trey puts his hand on my shoulder. I look at his hand and back up at him. Trey quickly moves his hand away. "There's supposed to be a raid at the Woodlawn spot tomorrow," he informs me.

"Okay, I'll have them clear out and move to the backup location tonight. Good looking out," I say to Trey as I give him dap.

When I make it to the kitchen, Cook quickly stands up and wipes her mouth as Eric zips his pants up.

"Are you fucking serious?" I slap the shit out of Cook. "Eric, you're supposed to be watching the security cameras. Cook, you can't cook crack with a dick in your mouth!" I scream.

Eric heads back to his designated area and resumes watching the cameras.

"I'm so sorry, Sonya. It'll never happen again," Cook cries.

"If you weren't one of the best cooks out here, I'd kill your stupid ass." I slap her again. "Get back to fucking work!" I bark at her and approach Eric. "If you're not watching the surveillance cameras and some jack boys or 5-0 want to catch us off guard and run up in here, they could. You know why? 'Cause you getting your little dick wet is more important," I yell in his face. "Now pick up the muthafuckin' walkie talkie and the damn gun and do your fucking job!" I scream.

"Walk me to my car, Trey," I order. We walk to the driver's side of my car and Trey opens my door for me. Before getting in the car, I instruct Trey to make Eric disappear and replace him with someone more reliable.

"Consider it done." Trey nods.

I put my shades on and get in my car. Now I have to go handle Ahmed. I swear my job is never done.

CHAPTER 6

Trey

One day Sonya will see the light and leave that clown Marques alone. I've loved her ever since we were children. My sister, Toya, and I had a rough childhood. Sonya always came through for us. When we had no food, she snuck some from her house and gave it to us. She gave Toya clothes and shoes from her closet. I love Sonya and she will always have my loyalty, no questions asked. When I was six, my pops decided not to return home from a trip to the local dope boy to get a hit. He accomplished getting my mom strung out before his disappearing act. Toya told me that before the crack came into our home, we had a normal childhood. I can only remember the struggle—pops gone and mom out on the streets trying to suck dick for a rock. I think that's why Toya is so fucked up in the head. She went through hell and had to learn how to survive at a young age, including trying to raise me. Toya is my heart; she protected me from harm, even if she had to put herself in harm's way.

Back to reality, I try to brainstorm on how I'm going to get rid of Eric's dumb ass. I walk back into the house and go into the kitchen.

"Cook, I need you to run to the Corner Store. Grab some drinks and snacks for everybody. Then hit up Rite Aide and get any supplies you might be running low on." I hand her three bills.

"Imma finish this batch then head right out," she says while stuffing the money in her pocket.

I nod in approval and reach for my phone to call Buck.

"Speak," he says.

"This Trey. I need you at the first spot," I tell him and he hangs up. Thirty minutes later, Cook is walking out the door. She spots a black van with blacked out windows pulling up. She looks at me then quickly walks off with her head down.

A short, dark skinned man exits the van followed by three tall, massive men. As they approach me, I study the short guy's face. His right eye is milky white; there are scares all over his face as if he'd been in a brutal knife fight. He has to be the ugliest nigga I'd ever seen; he was something out of a horror flick, but one of the deadliest niggas I know.

"Where and how many?" Buck asks.

"In the front, only one," I answer.

Buck and his three brothers enter the house, ready for work. I walk up behind them as they surround Eric. "Trey, what I do, bro?" Eric asks.

Buck gives Eric an injection in his neck to temporarily paralyze him.

"You fucked up big time. I hope the head was worth it. What Sonya says, goes. So you gotta go," I explain.

A lone tear trickles down his face.

"It's not personal, it's business. You knew what your job was and you failed," I say and give Buck a nod to let him know I was done.

Buck's three brothers snatch Eric up and carry him to the van. After loading him in, Buck turns to me and says, "I'll give him one to the dome, cut 'em up, bag 'em up, and then dump him in the Chesapeake Bay with some chains and cinder blocks." He holds his hand out and I hand him a manila envelope with thirty thousand. "Pleasure doing business with you," Buck says and disappears in his black death mobile.

I return inside the house and sit in Eric's spot to keep an eye on the security cameras. I need someone reliable to take Eric's old job, so I give my boy Ro a call.

"What's good, T?" Ro answers the phone.

"A position opened up. You still want a job?" I ask.

"Tell me where you need me and I'm there," he says.

"The first spot. I got everything you need. Leave your tool at home," I tell him and he hangs up. An hour later, Cook is in the kitchen doing her thing and Ro is sitting in Eric's spot.

***

Sonya

BZZZ. The door to Ahmed's office opens. When I enter, I see Ahmed sitting on the leather sofa with a terrified look on his face. Marques is sitting on the desk, cleaning his nails with a hunting knife, and taunting Ahmed. Ginger is sitting in the desk chair behind Marques. I walk up to Marques and kiss him passionately while staring at Ginger. After tonguing him down, I walk up to Ginger and tell her to get out of my seat.

"Your services are no longer needed at this time. You are dismissed," I tell her. Ginger speed walks out of the office, making sure to avoid looking at Marques.

I start going through Ahmed's desk. "So, I hear from my girl all the way in Louisiana, expecting her to be in a good mood. I just knew she was calling to tell me that she had a good flight and was happy to see her boo," I speak to nobody in particular. "Unfortunately, I get the total opposite. My best friend, my sister is irate. Angry!" I yell and slam my fist on the desk. Marques and Ahmed both jump from the noise.

"You want to know what she said, Ahmed?" I ask as I stand up and walk towards him. "Marques, hand me your piece. Hold on. I got my own," I say as I reach behind me and pull out my Beretta.

Ahmed begins to shake in fear.

"Don't you wanna know why she was upset?" I scream and begin to beat Ahmed with the butt of my gun. "Huh? I can't hear you, nigga! Speak the fuck up!" I continue to beat him.

"Sonya! Chill out, ma! You're going to kill him," Marques says as he grabs my arm.

I look down and see a bloody mess in front of me. "Fuck, I think I went too far this time," I tell Marques.

"You think? I can't recognize the muthafucka's face anymore," Marques says and shakes his head.

I begin to pace back and forth, trying to figure out how this half dead scumbag is going to come up with two hundred thousand by tomorrow. "Look at me, fat boy!" I kick Ahmed in the side. He lifts his head up as best as he can and looks at me with the eye that is not swollen shut. "This is what you're going to do. You will come up with two hundred by tomorrow afternoon. If you cannot come up with the money, you will sign over ownership of this fine establishment to Latoya Cummings," I instruct.

Ahmed nods his head and struggles to get up.

"Make whatever phone calls you gotta make, but you will not leave this office. Marques, cancel our reservations for dinner tonight because you're going to be babysitting Ahmed," I say in frustration.

CHAPTER 7

Sonya

I walk into Ahmed's bathroom to clean his blood off myself and the gun. Looking in the mirror, I flash back to the summer of 2001, the first time I took a life. I was only ten years old and so innocent. Toya and I had been best friends for two years.

"Mom. I'm going to Toya's," I yelled upstairs.

"Okay, honey. Make sure you're home before the street lights come on," she shouted back to me.

Before leaving, I grabbed a plastic bag and filled it with some food as quietly as I could and headed out the door. As I walked up to Toya's row house, her mom speed walked out the house, counting some crumpled bills. She didn't even notice me standing there as she continued to march towards a group of guys on the corner. I walked up the stairs and entered the house. It was dark and reeked of urine. I flipped the light switch but the lights didn't come on.

There was noise coming from upstairs, so I felt my way up the stairs, towards the noise. Once I made it to the final stair, Trey runs up to me, motioning for me to be quiet. When I saw his tear-streaked face, I realized that something wasn't right. Quietly, I entered Toya's room and noticed the dim glow of a metal flashlight pointing towards Toya's mattress. I froze in fear at the sight of a local dope boy grunting and sweating on top of her. Toya didn't see me standing in the doorway as she stared blankly at the flashlight. Is she dead? The pervert was so into what he was doing that he didn't notice me put down my bag and approach the flashlight.

All of a sudden, he jerked. "Fuck! Ugh! I'm cummin'."

I quickly grabbed the heavy metal flashlight and hit him in the head with all of my strength. He passed out on top of Toya and I tried rolling him off of her, but he's too heavy.

Toya still wasn't moving; I slapped her lightly on the cheek. "Toya, please, help me get him off you. Toya! Snap out of it!" I scream.

"Huh? Sonya, what you doing here?" Toya whispers.

"Help me get him off of you. I need you to push," I tell her.

We struggled for at least two minutes, but we finally got him off. Toya grabbed her ripped panties off the floor and threw them back down. She put her pants on and looked at me as she buttoned them.

"Go downstairs and get the sharpest thing you can find. Hurry up, before he wakes up," she instructed me.

I ran down the stairs and into the kitchen, grabbing the first thing I see and ran back up the stairs. "Stab him," Toya whispered.

I hesitate, terrified at the thought of killing someone. "If we don't kill him, he will wake up and kill all three of us," Toya said.

Trey was sitting in the corner of the room crying and rocking himself back and forth. Toya began to yell at me to stab him and he begins to move. The room started spinning and my hands began to shake. The palms of my hands were damp with sweat.

"Kill him, Sonya! Do it! Do it now!" Toya screamed.

I must have blacked out because all I remember was standing over that man's body with a bloody screwdriver in my hand. I dropped the screwdriver and looked at my hands in shock. It hit me that I had done it; I had killed someone.

"Here, take his shirt. Wipe off your face and your hands then wrap the screwdriver in the shirt. Trey, get up. We gotta get out of here before mom comes back," Toya ordered.

Trey got up and grabbed the flashlight, and then began screaming and beating the dead body in a rage. Releasing all of his anger and frustration, he beat the man's face beyond recognition. I grabbed Trey and all three of us ran out of the house. Instinctively, we ended up at my house. I quietly opened the door and peeked in. I could hear my mom in the kitchen cooking dinner. I waved Toya and Trey into the house.

"Mom! I'm home!" I yelled as the three of us ran upstairs.

"Okay, baby. Make sure you wash up before dinner," she shouted back.

When we made it to my room, we all dropped to the floor to catch our breath. I finally stood up and opened my closet. "Here, Toya. We wear the same size," I said as I tossed her a nightgown.

I went to my dresser to retrieve a pair of panties for Toya, some sweatpants for Trey, and a T-shirt as well. After getting what I needed for myself, I lead Toya and Trey to the bathroom. "Put your stuff on the sink and wait here," I told them.

I got to the closet in the hallway for some towels, washcloths, and soap. When I returned to the bathroom, I locked the door and filled the tub with warm water, and then we undressed. We've had to do this plenty of times in the past because Toya's mom could never keep the utilities on. We got into the tub together, me in the rear, Toya in the middle and Trey in the front. We washed off with our own washcloths, sharing the soap between the three of us. I'd wash Toya's back as she washed Trey's.

After our bath we dried off, got dressed, grabbed our dirty clothes and went back into my room. I noticed that Toya had left the bloody T-shirt, containing the screwdriver, on the floor. I hid it deep in my closet until I could figure out what to do with it. I picked at my food that night as Toya and Trey stayed in my room as quiet as mice. I wasn't hungry because of what had taken place a few hours earlier.

"May I be excused?" I asked.

"You've hardly touched your food," my mom said with a confused look on her face.

"I'm not hungry; I just want to get some rest," I reply.

"Okay, put your plate in the refrigerator, next to your dad's," my mom said.

After doing as I was told, my mom kissed me goodnight and I went to my room. Later that night, when I knew my mom was deep in her sleep, Toya, Trey, and I snuck downstairs and I made two peanut butter and jelly sandwiches for each of them. After they filled their bellies and drank some red Kool-Aid, we cleaned up and went to bed. Toya and I laid at the top of the bed and Trey laid at the foot. Toya didn't cry that night or any other time after that. I knew that holding all of her pain inside would eventually change her, but not in a good way.

***

Clyde

Mookie finally left and I was ready to get reacquainted with Toya's body. While she took a shower, I lit some scented candles in the room and put on some slow jams. After setting the mood, I join her in the shower. Without hesitation, I pin her against the wall and begin to kiss and trace my tongue from her neck, down to her breasts. Toya moans with pleasure as I suckle on her hard pink nipples and play with her clit.

"Lick that pussy daddy," she purrs.

"Who pussy this is?" I ask her.

"Yours, daddy," she moans.

"Who?" I ask again.

She speaks louder, "Yours, daddy! That's your pussy."

I smile and bite my bottom lip. I squat down and put one of her legs over my shoulder. I flick my tongue up and down, back and forth, driving her crazy. "You like dat?" I ask her.

"Yes baby, please don't stop," she begs.

I slide two fingers in her pussy and continue to suck on her clit. "Oh, my goodness! Daddy, yes!" she screams.

I slide my fingers out and place her other leg on my other shoulder, stand up, and lift her off her feet. I'm sucking and licking that sweet, pink pussy as she grabs the back of my head and grinds into me.

"I'm about to cum! Right there, baby. Keep doing that shit!" she growls. I continue to suck and lick the fuck out of that pussy. She begins to jerk. "I'm cumming, baby! I'm cumming!" Toya screams.

I don't let up on her; I keep up the pace.

"Baby, stop! Oh shit!" she screams and begins to squirm in my arms. "I can't no more, baby, please stop!" she screams and grabs her hair. I stop long enough to look up at her and laugh. She's panting.

"You asshole" she laughs.

"Oh, Imma asshole huh?" I ask and commence to suck on her swollen clit. I'm driving her bat shit crazy and loving it. Her body gets stiff and I feel the second burst of cream on my tongue.

Satisfied with what I did, I put Toya down slowly and help regain her composure. She kisses me passionately as I wrap my arms around her and wash her back. I soap her body down, making sure not to miss a spot as she washes me. Toya pays close attention to my dick, getting it nice and soapy while playing with it.

"You like that, daddy?" she purrs.

"Fuck yeah," I tell her. She rinses off and kneels down. "What you gonna do wit all dat?" I ask her with a smile.

Toya bites her lip and winks at me. Oh shit! She just engulfed all ten inches down her throat. "Fuck!" I yell as I move her hair from around her face.

It turns me on even more as I hold her hair, looking down at her and she's looking up at me. The slurping and gargling sounds she's making drives me insane. Toya reaches behind me and grabs my ass, pulling me and pushing, making me fuck her mouth.

"Oh, shit guh!" I look towards the ceiling.

Toya pulls my wood from her mouth and jerks me off as she tells me that she wants me to cum down her throat. She goes back to deep throating me. I feel it creeping up on me. My toes curl and I fuck her mouth faster and harder.

"Oh, shit! Ugh! Ugh! Ugh!" I cum deep down her throat. Toya swallows and smiles up at me. "Damn, guh. You da truth," I say as I try to catch my breath.

I don't know what it is about this girl, but I got hard again the moment she touched me. We got out of the shower, soaking wet. I lift her up and sit her on my dick. I'm making love to her, slow and deep, as I walk to the bedroom. She begins to grind on me as I hold her up, moaning and biting her bottom lip. Without pulling out, I place her on the edge of the bed and dig deep. Toya uses her right hand to play with her nipple as she bites on her finger on her left hand. She's holding in her screams so I fuck her harder and faster.

"Oooh, baby! You're making that pussy feel so good," she screams.

I feel a huge gush as she squirts all over the place. She turns around and I continue to knock the bottom out that pussy. Toya throws it back at me thrust for thrust. I'm growling and grunting; this shit feels so good. As I'm hitting it from the back, she lays flat on her stomach, never missing a beat. I can feel her throbbing and tightening around my dick.

"I'm cumming again!" she screams. Toya creams all over me then tells me to lay back. Toya straddles me and rides me nice and slow, moaning and playing with her nipples.

Sweat trickles down her thick, luscious body; the sight of her turns me on. I pull her face to mine and we kiss as she continues to ride me. She turns around and rides me reverse cowgirl. The harder and faster she goes, the more her ass claps. I grab her ass, bite my lip, and fuck her back.

"I'm 'bout to nut," I growl. Toya climbs off me and puts my dick on her tongue as I cum.

"Mmm, so sweet," she says with her mouth full. She shows me her tongue and swallows. Damn, I love this girl.

CHAPTER 8

Toya

After putting it on Clyde, we fell asleep in each other's arms. Three hours later, I woke up to the sound of Clyde talking to someone. I get out of bed, stretch, and put on Clyde's T-shirt. I wonder who he's talking to, so I walk towards his voice. When I reach the kitchen, I spot Clyde and some female laughing and talking. I just stand there watching them bump their gums. She's playfully hitting him on his chest and clucking at all his lame ass jokes. Instantly, my woman's intuition kicks in.

"Please give me a reason to gut this bitch," I say to myself.

I clear my throat loud enough for the both of them to hear me. They both turn around surprised and I notice how quickly Clyde puts some distance between him and Thotterella.

"Hey, bae. How long you been up?" Clyde asks.

"I just woke up. Aren't you going to introduce me to your little friend?" I reply.

Did this bitch just smirk at me? I suddenly get the urge to bitch slap that smug ass grin off her face. "Oh! This my cousin, Michelle," Clyde answers nervously.

"Umhmm. I bet," I say and roll my eyes. "Michelle, dis my guh, Toya."

Michelle walks up to me and tries to shake my hand, but I look at it like it's contaminated. "Nice to meet you. I done heard so much about you. I could write a book," Michelle says.

"Funny. I can't say the same about you, Mitchel," I reply with much attitude.

"Bae, bae! I don't know who done pissed in yo cereal, but you got da wrong one. Trust, you don't want dis problem," Michelle says as she rolls her neck.

I start to laugh in her face hysterically. "This bitch can't even speak proper English," I say in between laughs.

I stop laughing abruptly and stare at her. She looks uncomfortable, shifting her weight from one foot to the other. I smile from ear to ear and stretch out my arm to shake her hand. "Girl, I was just fucking with you! Any family of Clyde's is family to me as well," I say pleasantly. "As a matter of fact, give me a hug."

I reach out to hug her. Michelle hugs me back and when she tries to let go, I squeeze her and whisper in her ear, "Trust and believe, if I find out there's some funny shit going on between you and MY man, I'm going to make you wish that you never met a bitch like me." I smile and let her go.

I can smell the fear seeping out her pores and my pussy instantly gets wet. "I'm hungry, baby. Can we go grab something to eat?" I ask Clyde as I continue to stare at Michelle.

"Yeah, we can go out for some grub," he replies.

"Good, cause all that freaky love making got me starving. I have to reenergize for round three," I say and wink at Michelle.

"Well, Imma head on out den. Call me when you got time, cuz," Michelle says to Clyde.

"Aight, kinfolk. We'll link up soon." Clyde heads to the door to let her out.

"Bye Michelle! It was so nice meeting you, honey!" I wink at her and wave.

Mental note to self, investigate this situation between Clyde and his 'cousin'. I head to the bathroom to brush my teeth and wash my face. Afterwards, I go through my luggage to pick out something comfortable to wear. I pull out some short shorts, a white tank top, and my metallic gold Jordans. Clyde put on a starched down pair of black Gucci jeans, a white tank top, and some gold special edition Space Jams. I put my hair in two big cornrows, some big gold hoops in my ears and a gold name plate chain.

"Damn, you lookin' good, bae," Clyde admires me from the bathroom doorway. "Thanks, boo. You're not so bad yourself," I reply as I put on my gold-framed Gucci shades. "So where are we going?" I ask him.

"Imma show you 'round A-Town, den we can grab somethin' to eat," Clyde says.

We get in the car and head out for an evening of sightseeing. "We live in Landmark," Clyde explains.

We soon arrive at a neighborhood by a Big Lots. I take in the scenery; there were a few decent houses, and a lot of ran down houses.

"Dis is da Nawfside," Clyde says.

We drive past some shabby apartments called Sunset that has a run down corner store across the street. Clyde continues to drive down Monroe Street. "Dis da home of the M.S.H., Monroe Street Hustlas. You might be interested in doing business wit dem," he tells me.

I make a mental note to myself about this so-called gang called M.S.H. We reach a light and take a left. "Imma take you to Kellyland. It's low key," Clyde says.

After leaving Kellyland we hit I-49.

"Dis is Willow Glen, one of da oldest streets on da Sawfside," Clyde explains and honks at some guys on the corner of 15th Street. We turn left on 6th Street. "Da niggas on dis street ain't to be fucked wit. They put in work."

I make sure to make a mental note about the 6th Street niggas as well. Next, I see a subdivision that actually looks pretty nice. "Dis is Riverbend Subdivision. High rent, a lot of rules. No charcoal grills allowed, no pools, not even da tiny ones for little kids, no trampoline. Basically, dey strict as hell and charge low-income families an arm and a leg," Clyde laughs.

We get to a stop sign, turn right, and hit 3rd Street. Clyde takes a right onto 3rd. "Imma take you to Acadian Village. Dis is where all da rich black folks lived during segregation," he explains as we pass an elementary school. When we leave Acadian, Clyde goes back up 3rd Street and turns left onto Douglas Street.

"Douglas Street, all da way up to Broadway Avenue is called da bottom side." Clyde slowly drives past some children playing in the street. We turn on a road that leads us to a bunch of schools. "Dat is W.O. Hall." Clyde points toward a small ran down school that had seen better days and should have been rebuilt years ago.

"Dat is Arthur F. Smith Middle School." He points across the street from the elementary school. The building looked a little better than the elementary school, but not by much. "And dis right here is Peabody Magnet High School." Clyde points to the right as he approaches a light. "The high school must get all the funding in this area, 'cause the other schools I've seen look outdated and run down," I tell him.

Clyde nods in agreement.

CHAPTER 9

Sonya

After a drink of Henny with coke, I call Buck and his brothers. "Speak," a raspy voice answers.

"I'm on my way to you. Stay put," I tell him and hang up. I make one more call to my Woodlawn spot.

"What's good, boss number two?" Chance says into the phone.

"The exterminator is coming to spray for roaches. Make sure y'all are packed up and moved out A.S.A.P.," I tell him.

"I got you, yo," Chance says and hangs up.

Done with making my phone calls, I get in my car and head to Charles Village to meet up with Buck. Once I get to my destination, I get out of my car and see a familiar face. "Ms. Cummings, how are you?" I ask.

"Sonya? Is that you? Hey, baby! I'm fine, still taking it one day at a time," she says.

"We are really proud of you for getting clean," I tell her as I give her a hug.

"God is definitely good. Have you heard from Toya and Trey?" she asks.

"You know Toya moved to Louisiana and Trey is always busy," I answer.

"I told that girl not to move down there. She has no family down there. I gotta bad feeling about it," she complains. "At least I know my baby, Trey, is doing good. Got that good job and staying outta trouble. I'm so proud of him, taking the right path in life," she says with pride.

"Well, you take care of yourself, Ms. Cummings. I have an appointment," I tell her.

"Alright, don't be a stranger," she tells me and continues to walk down the sidewalk.

"If only she knew what Trey does with his free time," I say to myself.

I walk into Buck's business, straight to the back where his office is. "Come in," Buck's raspy voice says through the door. "Have a seat," Buck says as I enter the smoky office.

I sit down across from his desk; the room is dimly lit and it's completely dark behind his desk. All I can see is the orange glow of his cigar.

"Buck, you need to chill out on the cigars. They stink to high hell," I tell him.

He laughs and leans forward so I can see his hideous face. He gets straight to business. "So, what brings one of my favorite clients here today?" he asks.

"I'm heading to Castlewood Road to take out some garbage. I'm in need of your cleaning services," I tell him.

"That'll cost you extra," Buck says.

"Put it on our tab," I say to him and smirk. When our meeting came to an end, Buck and his brothers started to load a van. Once everything was packed, they climb into the van and follow me to our destination.

By the time we arrive, it's dark outside and the streets lights are on. I make sure to park down the street from Ahmed's house and slip on an Islamic Abaya Jilbab. I know that his wife will most likely let me in with it on. I make sure that my 45 has one in the chamber and conceal it. Then I remove the battery from one of my phones so it will seem as though the battery died. Finally, I call Toya on my throw away to let her know what's going on and she instructs me on what to do and to keep her on the line. So I hide the phone in my back pocket to where she can hear everything.

I nod at Buck to let him know it's game time. I head to the door quickly, my adrenaline pumping. Buck and his brothers hide on the side of the house and wait for my signal. I knock on the door and wait, but no one answers. I ring the doorbell and hear somebody approaching the door. A beautiful woman answers the door. She's about five feet, seven inches in height, with golden skin, dark eyes, long thick lashes, full lips and a nice frame from what I could tell. She kind of resembled the late, great Aaliyah.

"Excuse me, I'm so sorry for bothering you. My car broke down and I need to call my husband. My phone battery is dead," I say and hold up my phone.

"Come in, come in," she waves me in and locks the door behind me. "I'll go get the phone for you," she says and walks away, leaving me by the door.

I wonder how someone so pretty and pleasant could end up with Ahmed's short, fat, hairy ass. I can hear cartoons playing on TV. I'm guessing the children are in the living room. I pull out my gun and wait for the woman's return.

"Here's the..." she stops talking and freezes in her steps. I put my finger up to my lips, signaling for her to keep quiet. Ahmed's wife follows my instructions when I wave my gun at her to come closer, making sure that I grab her phone out of her hand. I reach behind me and unlock the door, never taking my eyes off of her. Buck and his brothers speed walk to me after I wave them in. Buck's horrifying face brings the woman to tears. She doesn't know who Buck is, but she would soon find out. I turn her around and push her towards the living room.

Buck whistles and admires his surroundings; everything is white and gold. The carpet looks like a thick bed of snow, the furniture was all white leather with gold decorative pillows, and the coffee table and end tables are glass with gold framing. It's impressive. Both of the kids look away from the TV and focus on us.

"Go sit down with your children," I tell her.

She walks to the couch and embrace her son and daughter, clinging to them for dear life. "What do you want? You can take anything, just please leave us alone," the woman begs.

I hold my finger up for her to wait a minute. I make a phone call, using the phone that I had took from Ahmed's wife, and toss her the phone. She doesn't waste any time ranting and crying into the phone. I snatch the phone from her and hear Ahmed crying on the other end.

"Put Marques on the phone," I order him.

"Who's this?" Marques asks.

"It's me, Sonya. Look, I'm at Ahmed's house preparing for the surprise party. Go ahead and get the paperwork done. When you're done, come join us for the party," I tell him.

"I'm on it. We'll be there in a minute," he says. I hang up the phone and wait for Marques, so we can begin the festivities.

***

Trey

It's been a long day and I can't wait to get home. I send Corey, Dro, and Ro home and instruct Dee, Booker, and Fred on what needs to be done. My replacement, Nico and I take a look around together as I give him a rundown on today's events.

"Damn, I sure hate that for Eric. He was dumber than a box of rocks, but he was good people," Nico says.

"Yeah, well, that's the business," I say and give Nico dap. "Aight, I'm out, son. I'm tired and smell like a trap house." I laugh and head out the door.

As I drive home, I admire my city and all of the lights. Baltimore looks amazing at night, especially from the Harbor. Home of the Ravens and Orioles, there's no city like it. If I want to go out of town, I'm not too far from D.C., Philly, New York, New Jersey, Richmond or Virginia Beach. Bmore isn't perfect; it has it's problems, just like any big city, but I wouldn't trade it for any other place.

Home sweet home. I pull into the parking garage and park next to my work vehicle, anxious to take a long, hot shower. As soon as I step into my condo, I turn on the news and head to my room. As I'm undressing, I hear something on the news that catches my attention. Dressed in nothing but my boxers, I return to the den to catch the news.

"Jim, what we know so far is that he was a well-known prosecutor from New Orleans. His family has been notified of the incident. We can now release his name. Thirty-seven year old Joshua Douzart, married, and the father of three children. This horrible act took place mid air, so the FBI will be investigating the homicide. Right now, there are no leads on who may have done this evil deed. The FBI and chief of police will be giving a news conference shortly. Back to you, Jim," the report says.

I don't hear anything after that. My mind begins to race a mile a second. As I pace my den back and forth, I call my sister.

"Hey, baby brother! Sorry, I haven't called. I've been a little tied up," Toya says.

"I'm not tripping on that. I'm just calling to see if you're okay. Anything you want to tell me, maybe?" I ask her.

"I'm fine, bro. You worry too much," she says.

"Have you watched the news?" I ask her.

"Haven't had time to watch anything. Why? What's up Trey?" Toya asks.

"Some lawyer from New Orleans was murdered on a flight from Baltimore," I tell her. It gets really quiet on the other end of the phone. Shit! I knew it. I know my sister. "Latoya Charmaine Cummings, please tell me it ain't so," I plead.

She starts laughing hysterically as if I told the best joke of the century.

"Stop playing, Tee. You know you can tell me anything. We don't keep secrets from each other, sis," I tell her. The laughing stops and I can hear her breathing on the phone. "Toya!" I yell.

"Alright, alright! He deserved it, Trey! He started it when he pushed me down while I was on the plane. I made sure he went out with a bang though," she boasts.

"Dammit, girl! Why can't you control your damn self? Why are you so damn extra? Fuck! I can't make this go away, sis. It's out of my reach; the FBI is all over it," I tell her.

"I covered my tracks. No worries, bro. It's all good, trust me," Toya says.

We talk a little while longer about Louisiana and how she's excited to be there. Afterwards, we say our goodbyes and I love yous and hang up. I'm sick with worry; Lord knows what she did to that man. Toya always takes shit to the extreme. I love my sister to death, but she needs to be in a padded room somewhere. Finally, I take a shower, letting the water wash away all of my stress. After the shower, I dress for bed and lay out what I was going to wear the next day, plus my suit for work tomorrow night.

CHAPTER 10

Clyde

On our way home from a night of fun, Toya received a bunch of phone calls. Her mood changed with each call. One minute she's excited, then laughing like a lunatic, to a blank stare and silence. I don't know how to take her mood swings, but I'm not surprised by them. The craziest bitches always have the best pussy. When we get to the house, Toya takes a shower and I check my text messages.

> *I miss you bae.*
> *When I'm gonna c u*
> *Y u ain't text me back yet?*
> *Fuck it. Have fun wit dat bitch*
> *If u don't text me back I'm comin to yo house*

I shake my head and text this girl back.

> *Just got home. Will talk to u tomorrow*

The water stops running in the shower so I delete the texts before Toya comes in the room. She walks in with a towel wrapped around her and a bottle of pear-scented lotion. I pat on the bed for her to lay down and take the bottle out of her hand. I apply lotion to every inch of her body and massage her to sleep.

While Toya is knocked out, I go in the bathroom and turn on the shower. As the water runs, I make a call to my sidepiece. "What you want Clyde?" she answers with attitude.

"Don't start dat bullshit. Why you trippin'?" I ask her.

"Boy, boo! Ain't nobody trippin'. I just know dat if you text me, you expect me ta answer right back, but you act like yo ass can't do da same," she complains.

"Mane, you is trippin'. I done told yo ass dat my guh was comin' in town. I'm doin' yo ass a favor by not textin' you right back. Do you know what dis guh will do if she find out anything?" I ask.

"I don't know and frankly, I don't give two flyin' fucks! Dat bitch don't want it wit me, real muthafuckin' talk. Nigga, you got me all da way fucked up!" she yells into the phone.

"Bring yo stupid ass ova here if ya want to. Don't say I ain't warn yo ass. Once you decide to pop up, it's outta my hands," I warn.

The bitch hangs up on me. Oh, well. She'll be aight. After taking a hot shower, I go to bed and admire Toya's naked body. I wanna fuck her so bad, but I know she's had a long day and needs her rest. Instead, I pull the blanket down from under her and climb into bed. Within ten minutes, I was knocked out, holding Toya in my arms. Surprisingly, I wake up in the morning to my sidepiece sucking the soul out of my dick. I look to my left and Toya isn't there.

"Oh, shit," I mumble as I look down at this girl putting in work like a pro. Before I could nut, she moves up to my chest, kissing and licking.

"What you doin', Michelle? My guh could be back any minute," I say to her, but she keeps going.

Michelle climbs on top of me and rides me slowly, tightening her walls. She's teasing me, just riding the head. My eyes roll back and Michelle picks up the pace, bringing me to the point of no return. "Cum wit me, nigga," she moans.

"What?" I ask, looking at her in shock.

"Shit! I'm cumming. Cum with me, Clyde," she moans.

I explode deep inside of her. Then she punches the shit out of me. I jump up, ready to defend myself. That's when I realize that I fucked up big time. It's still dark outside and Michelle is gone. I was dreaming; it was Toya the whole time. I was calling her Michelle. Fuck my life.

***

Sonya

Finally, the doorbell rings and one of Buck's brothers goes to answer the door. He returns with Marques and Ahmed in tow. Ahmed tries to run to his wife and kids but Marques snatches him by the collar of his shirt and holds him back.

"Andalah, I'm so sorry this is happening," Ahmed cries to his wife. She looks down, crying with disappointment.

"Okay, okay. Enough of the theatrics. You two." I point towards the kids. "Stay here on the couch. Buck, you stand behind them and keep an eye on them," I order. "Andalah, or whatever your name is. Come sit over here on the loveseat," I tell her.

She gets up, kisses the children, and does as she's told.

"Ahmed, you can stand right there with Marques," I instruct. "Marques, did you finalize the paperwork?" I ask.

"All the T's are crossed and I's are dotted," he responds.

"Good. Now tell your wife why we are gathered here tonight, Ahmed," I demand. Ahmed tells his wife about his drug-infused party, him fucking a stripper, and losing money.

Andalah puts her face into her hands and cries harder. Her kids begin to scream and cry at the sight of their mother breaking down. "These kids are too damn loud," I complain.

BANG! BANG! Both of the bastards slump over dead. Two of Buck's brothers are standing behind the couch with guns drawn.

"Nasra! Nasir! No!" Ahmed screams and tries to break away from Marques' grip. Andalah is rocking back and forth, praying to Allah, but stops and becomes completely quiet. Clearly, she's in shock. I look at Buck's brothers like they're crazy.

"What? You said they was too loud. Shit, the little fuckers were getting on our nerves too," one of them say.

I shake my head. "I wasn't ready for y'all to shoot them yet. Dang!" The sight of her children's blood and brain matter all over the white leather and snow white carpet sends her over the edge. Andalah tries to charge towards me but is cut short with my fist breaking her nose.

I put my arm around her neck and place my Beretta to her temple. "Uh, uh, uh! Don't try nothing stupid. Besides, the fun is just beginning," I tell her. "Buck, come strip her down."

I push her down to the carpet.

"Gladly," Buck rasps and licks his lips.

"No! No! No! Please!" Ahmed yells and he tries to fight his way to his wife. Marques shuts him down with two jabs to the jaw, dislocating it. Buck rips Andalah's clothing off until she is completely naked. "You are one bad bitch. Ahmed, your wife has a nice body."

"Marques make him kneel next to her," I order.

Marques pushes him down to his knees. I know Buck is one ugly ass nigga, so I know pussy don't come easy unless he's paying for it.

"Yo, Buck. Did she insult you with the way she looked at you, when you and your brothers first came into the house?" I ask.

"Yeah, she did," Buck's brother answers.

"Don't you have something special to show her?" I ask Buck.

Without saying anything, Buck looks at his brothers. All three of them approach Andalah and hold her down. Buck pulls his pants down anxiously and pulls his dick out of his boxers. "Hold her other leg down, Ahmed," I demand. Marques puts his gun to the back of Ahmed's head and he complies.

Andalah looks at Buck in shock. I bet she's terrified of the size and how he is going to fit that all in her. Buck hocks up some spit in his hand to lubricate himself and rams into her. He starts to drool as her screams gas him up. As Buck has his little fun, I pull my phone from my back pocket and lay it on the end table. Knowing it'll take awhile, I grab a magazine off the coffee table and get comfortable. Half way through the magazine, I glance at my Rolex. Forty-five minutes passed when Buck finally got his rocks off. Drenched in sweat, Buck stands up and pulls his pants up. His brothers take turns violating every hole on her body. After the deed is done, I grab Andalah off of the floor and tie her to a chair.

"Did you enjoy the show, Ahmed?" I ask.

"You bitch! I'm going to kill you!" Ahmed screams.

"Aww. I thought you would enjoy it. Isn't it better than a strip tease?" I ask. He doesn't say anything, just looks at me with pure hate in his eyes. "Let me enlighten you a bit. Everything that's taking place tonight was planned by Toya. I apologize for how creative she can be. Personally, I would have shot all of you and went home," I say.

Marques laughs. "That damn Toya is a savage. Straight up beast mode on that ass," he jokes.

"Now, where were we? Oh! I remember," I snap my fingers. "Toya, you still there?" I ask as I pick the phone up from the end table.

"Keep going," Toya whispers into the phone.

"You heard the boss. She wants us to keep going." I smirk.

I tell Marques to take out his hunting knife. Andalah's eyes are wide with terror as she looks at the blade of the knife.

"Don't worry, that's not for you," I tell her. "Ahmed, your greedy ass nose has put your family in a jam. It's so unfortunate that they have to suffer for your fuck up. Marques, would you like to have the honor?" I ask.

"I don't mind at all if I do." He smiles.

Marques cuts off Ahmed's nose and holds it up for all to see. Ahmed is bleeding profusely, holding his face, and calling Marques every name that his mind could conjure up. Buck's brother takes Ahmed's nose from Marques and approaches Andalah.

"That nose is the reason your children are dead," I tell her. Marques grabs Ahmed's hair and forces him to look at his wife. I nod at Buck's brother and he jams Ahmed's nose into Andalah's mouth. "Eat up." I tap my gun on her cheek.

She chews and gags, chews and gags. "Good girl, now swallow. Not polite to play with your food." I pat her on the head.

After swallowing, she begins to choke. Her lips begin to turn purple.

"Don't die on me yet. I'm not done with you," I say and gut punch her as hard as I can. Andalah vomits all over the floor and herself. "Okay, let's wrap this up guys. I'm tired," I tell Buck and his brothers.

Buck opens up his bag of goodies and pulls out some hedge clippers. One by one, he snips off Andalah's fingers and toes. She screams in agony, and Ahmed faints. Marques slaps him to wake him up.

"Wake up, Ahmed. You'll miss all of the fun. Toya was nice enough to give you front row tickets and this is the thanks you give her, by falling asleep?" I ask.

Next, Buck pulls out some fishhooks and hooks them all over Andalah's breasts. She can no longer take the pain and passes out. Lastly, Buck pulls out a thirteen-inch steel dildo with razor sharp spikes. He wastes no time brutally raping her with it. This is some of the most gruesome shit I have ever seen. I feel sick to my stomach, but keep my composure. Andalah sits in that chair mutilated, bloody, and dead. Her cold, dead eyes stare at Ahmed.

"Any last words. Ahmed?" I ask.

"You'll all burn in hell for this! All of you will burn! Just kill me. I have nothing left to live for!" he screams.

Marques puts a bullet in Ahmed's head and shrugs. "I'll take them to the crematorium then dump their ashes in the Chesapeake."

"Toya wants you to chop up the kids, box them up, wrap them with a bow, and leave them at Ahmed's parents' doorstep," I tell them.

Toya hangs up without saying a word. I have seen firsthand, the evil things that she is capable of, but at this very moment I realize how sadistic my best friend really is.

CHAPTER 11

Toya

The sound of blood curdling screams turned me on so much that I couldn't keep from touching myself. I hang up on Sonya and take full advantage of Clyde's body. I was enjoying myself until this fool started talking in his sleep. I knew it! That bitch wasn't his cousin. It's cool though; I can handle the situation some other time. I climb on top of Clyde and ride him into pure ecstasy. Clyde and I explode together, and then I punch him dead in his face. He jumps out of bed ready to fight, standing there dumbfounded.

"Yeah, it's me. You know, your girlfriend, Toya!" I say as I get out of the bed. "Cat got your tongue nigga?" I scream in his face.

"Bae, it's not what you think," he says.

"Sshhh. Now, now. No need to explain. I'm willing to sweep this one infraction under the rug because I truly love you," I say sweetly as I rub my hand against his cheek.

"Damn, bae. You down for a nigga for real." Clyde smiles.

"Besides, I heard you while you were talking to her in the bathroom. I'm surprised that I'm not even mad about it. It doesn't fuck with my money," I tell him.

Clyde looks at me suspiciously and I laugh. "I'm serious. As a matter of fact, I'm willing to make amends with Michelle and we can even share her." I smile.

The mention of a threesome both shocked and enticed him.

"I see somebody is happy about that little arrangement." I look down.

"I love yo ass, guh!" Clyde strokes himself.

"Show me how much you love my ass." I wink and turn around on all fours. Clyde gently kisses both of my ass cheeks and smacks them. I arch my back in anticipation and look back at him. We made love until the sun came up. That morning Sonya called me on three-way with Trey.

"Good morning, my loves," I greet both of them.

They both say their hellos and we get down to business. "Woodlawn?" I ask Sonya.

"Successful move," she replies.

"Park Heights?" I ask Trey.

"Smooth sailing. Had to let Eric go. I gave Ro the job," Trey says.

"I'm not surprised about Eric. Harford County?" I ask.

"Marques and I was a little tied up with that surprise party. We'll get on that," Sonya says. "What about our little business transaction with the Arab?" I ask.

"Everything is signed. You should be receiving the paperwork in the mail within a week," Sonya replies.

"Did the cleaning crew do a good job of cleaning after the party?" I ask Sonya.

"Spic and span," she says.

"Good. Beast and Sincere will be dropping by from New York today. Make sure that's done before you start your shift tonight," I tell Trey.

"Bet, I'm headed out now. Call me later, sis. Love ya," he says and hangs up.

"Sonya, I appreciate you taking care of everything while I'm here," I tell her.

"I got some big shoes to fill. Don't know how you did it all, but I got your back, sis," Sonya says.

"This will pay off soon; stay focused. You got Marques and Trey to help you, use them. I'm going to buy a car today. Clyde and I are going to some club tonight. Hopefully I'll run into some business prospects and some of the competition," I tell her.

"Sounds like a plan. Be careful down there, sis. You're not in Bmore anymore. New stomping grounds, new people, and new problems," Sonya says.

"I can handle whatever they throw at me. They need to watch out for me." I laugh.

"I love you girl!" Sonya says.

"Love you too. Talk to you soon. Bye." I hang up.

Knowing that Trey and Sonya are taking care of things back home puts me at ease. As I pick out my outfit for the day, Clyde tells me that he needs to make a quick run and will be right back. He leaves out the door and locks it behind him. As I lotion up my body, someone knocks on the door.

"Hold on!" I yell while putting my robe on. When I get to the door, I look through the peephole. Clyde's friend is standing on the other side. I let my hair down and loosen the belt to my robe, then open the door. "Hey, Monkey. How are you?" I ask with a smile.

"It's Mookie." He laughs nervously. Mookie looks me up and down, and then looks away. "Oh! My bad, Mookie. What's up?" I ask.

"Clyde here?" he asks. "I gotta holla at him."

"Do you see his car outside?"

"Now that you mention it, I don't. Damn, my fault." He blushes.

"It's cool. I'll tell him you came by," I tell him. I 'accidentally' knock my hand against the belt on my robe and it opens up, exposing my naked body to Mookie.

"Damn, guh. You make a nigga wanna snatch you up," he says.

"Oh, shit! I'm so sorry," I apologize and quickly tie up my robe.

"Don't be sorry," Mookie says as he bites his lip and grabs his crotch.

I smile and close the door in his face. By the time Clyde gets home, I'm dressed in an all white Prada pantsuit that hugs my curves, with some gold peeptoe stilettos, gold bangles, diamond studs in my ears, and a gold rope chain. I top off the outfit with some gold-framed glasses to give me a professional look. Clyde looks at me, appreciating my beauty, and kisses me.

"Where we headed, bae?" he asks.

"Car shopping. I need some wheels," I reply.

"What kinda car you want?"

"Nothing special; something that won't stand out. I don't want to get the attention of the cops," I tell him.

I grab my white leather briefcase and we head out to do some car shopping. Clyde takes me on MacArthur Drive first. As soon as we step out of the car, a dealer approaches us immediately. It's like they smell big money, like sharks to blood.

"How ya doin'? Name's Jim Bob, at your service. What can I help ya with?" the dealer asks.

I hold in my laugh at what stood before me. He was a tall, midnight black man with a suit, cowboy boots, and a cowboy hat on. He even had one of those belts with the huge buckle on it. This brotha was beyond country.

I clear my throat. "Um, yes, you can help me. I want to see all of your latest models. No trucks please," I tell him.

"Well, you came to the right place, ma'am. Is there a pacific color you want? Pacific size maybe?" he asks.

"Yes, as a matter of fact I do have a SPECIFIC color in mind," I elaborate.

Clyde nudges me. He can see tears welling up in my eyes. I'm trying so hard not to bust out laughing.

"I prefer white or red, nothing too small. Plenty of room in the trunk," I tell him.

"I got a few cars in mind for ya. Follow me to ya future car." Black cowboy leads us to a white Ford Edge. I give him a flat out no. "Okay. Movin' right along," he says.

After an hour on the car lot, I finally decided on an all white Expedition.

"Alrighty, ma'am. Let's draw up the paperwork and getcha on thee road." Brotha cowboy leads us to his desk. "So uh, how much will ya be puttin down on it today?" he asks.

I place my briefcase on his desk, open it, and turn it towards him, "All of it."

His eyes bulge out of his head. "Well you came prepared huh? That's what I'm talkin' 'bout! A nigga 'bout to get a big check for dis deal."

What happened with the whole corny ass cowboy act? This nigga just got really hood on me. I smile and sign all of the necessary paperwork.

"Pleasure doing business with you." I shake his hand. "Oh, and you can keep the briefcase. There should be a nice tip in there as well."

"Good lookin' out. I 'preciate da tip; we gotta look out for our own kind. Know what I'm sayin?" he said.

I shake my head and walk out the building, a new car owner.

Clyde asks me where I need to go next. "I need to put a lawyer on retainer. Any good ones in mind?" I ask him.

"There's Bridgette Green. You'll have to call and set up an appointment wit her," he says.

We get in our cars and I follow Clyde back home. Once we get in the house, I kick off my heels and head to the bar. As I pour myself a shot of patron, I notice Clyde staring at me. After swallowing the liquid fire, I ask him why is looking at me like that.

"I just can't believe how lucky I am, bae. You handle business, don't take shit from nobody, willing to bring anotha bitch into our bed, and know how to play ya cards right."

I nod in agreement; he is right, but forgot one crucial detail.

***

Mookie

That bitch got something up her sleeve. She made sure that I saw her naked, now I want her even more. Evil, smart, and cunning. I like that shit. Just thinking about her got my dick on rock.

My girl walks in the den. "What you want me ta cook fa dinner?"

I walk up to her and push her onto the couch. "Bae, what you doin?" she asks. I force her to bend over and push her face into the couch. "Mookie, you hurtin' me. I can hardly breath!"

I smack her in the back of her head. "Shut da fuck up." As she cries, I place my elbow in the small of her back to make her arch. "You gone take dis dick and you better enjoy it." I smack her ass as hard as I can. "What you say?"

"Yes, daddy!" she screams.

I remove my belt from my pants and force them down. Grabbing a handful of her weave and holding the belt in my other hand, I ram into her, showing no mercy. I don't give a fuck if it hurts or feels good to her. "Throw it back, bitch!" I hit her ass with the belt. She complies to my demands, scared of the consequences.

"Aww shit, Toya! This pussy so damn good. Ugh!" I groan and hit her with the belt again. On the verge of busting, I yank her up by her weave and force her to her knees. I drop the belt and grab her face with both hands. I rape her face as she chokes and gags. "Bitch, if you throw up, Imma beat yo ass," I threaten.

Tears start rolling down her cheeks, so I pull out and smack her with my dick. "Say you want daddy dick," I demand.

"I...I...want daddy dick," she cries. I spit in her face and slap the piss outta her, pissed off that she's fucking up my fantasy.

"Stop all dat bitch ass cryin' and suck dis dick like you love it or I swear Imma tie yo ass up and beat you till I get tired," I growl.

I pry her mouth open with my hands and commence to fuck her mouth. "Suck dat shit, Toya. I know you been wantin' dis dick. Ugh, fuck yeah! Take dat shit!"

The thought of Toya's body made me go harder and faster. "Look at me bitch and take dis nut."

She looks up at me as I release all over her face. Sweating profusely and gasping for air, I pull up my pants and look at her with disgust. "Go clean yoself up. You look like shit."

I push her to the floor, grab my keys, and walk out the door. Clyde thinks he did me a favor by hooking me up with his sister. It was alright when I first got out of jail and needed a place to crash. Now I want something else, something new, and something much better. Toya came right on time; she doesn't know it yet, but she's going to love me.

I pull up to Clyde's house and head to the door. I notice a brand new Expedition in the driveway. This nigga bought her a car. How do I compete with that? He always made sure I was beneath him by giving me crumbs; he got me out here nickel and diming. He'll get his, best believe that. I ring the doorbell and Clyde answers.

"What it do, my nigga?" I greet him and give him dap.

"Come in, bo." He holds the door open.

As soon as I enter the house, my eyes connect with Toya's ass. Damn, she looks good in that white suit. "Hey, Ms. Toya. How ya doin?"

She smiles at me and takes a shot of some clear liquor. A woman of few words, my kinda girl.

Clyde puts his hand on my shoulder. "How 'bout we go talk in my office." I follow Clyde to one of the spare rooms that he had turned into an office. As soon as he closes the door, he grabs me by my shirt, "What I told you 'bout lookin' at my guh like dat bruh?"

I push his ass off of me and straighten out my shirt. "First of all, don't put yo hands on me, nigga. You should be happy that you got a guh that niggas look at. Take that shit as a compliment, bo."

Clyde's nose flares as he mean mugs me. He must think I'm scared of him. Cute. I walk to one of his chairs and sit down.

"Anyway, I came by to tell you that I got a lick. It will benefit the both of us," I say.

Clyde takes a seat in his chair. "Aight, well what is it?"

I knew the mention of a good deal and more money would reel his ass in. "I got some people out in Fort Worth that got the hook up on some beans."

"What kind they got?" he asks.

"He got some Percocet, Xanax, roxies, narcos, all kinds of shit, even some bar."

Clyde sits up in his seat, excited by the news. "What's da ticket?" he asks.

I rub my hands together. "He willing to trade. Cans for green."

Clyde goes deep into thought, doing the math in his head. "It sounds like a good deal. A little too good. Let me holla at my connect and I'll get back to you on dat."

We stand up and give each other dap. "Aight, I'm gone, bruh. Yo sister been trippin' lately. Get back to me on that situation soon."

I leave Clyde in his office and head towards the door. On the way out, I look Toya up and down and wink at her. Toya winks back and licks her lips seductively. "Aight, Ms. Toya. It was nice seeing you again."

I smile and close the door behind me. When I get in my car, I spot Toya in the window staring at me. I'mma get you one day, watch and see. I pull off with my dick on hard. I was gonna go get a drink, but decided on going home to fuck this bitch again, wishing it was Toya.

CHAPTER 12

Marques

After last night's festivities, I decided to take a day to myself. That shit was bananas. Sonya surprised the hell out of me. I never knew she could be so ruthless. Now that I think about it, I shouldn't be shocked when Toya's pulling all the strings. I have a craving for some Hooters wings, so I drive to the Inner Harbor to grab a bite to eat. As I'm enjoying my food, a call comes through. I look at the caller I.D.

"Shit." I quickly prepare myself for this girl's bullshit and answer the phone. "Speak." The first thing I hear is a bunch of hoodrats cackling, kids playing, loud music, and a car alarm going off in the background.

"What the hell happened to you the other day, Marques?" Keisha screams into the phone. This bitch is trying to put on a show for her friends. "What the fuck I told you about calling me on some dumb shit, Keisha?"

She sucks her teeth. "I know you not getting loud wit' me. You stood ME up, remember?" she yells.

Her friends are in the background instigating. "Matter fact nigga, fuck you! Imma bad bitch and if you wanna play games, you can kiss my muthafuckin' ass!" Keisha screams.

"Keep on..." I started to speak, but she cut me off.

"Hold on Marques. Jaquarius and Mercedes! Get ya asses out the street and stay on the sidewalk or Imma whoop that ass," she screams at two of her kids.

I have to keep reminding myself why I keep dealing with this sewer rat. "Good pussy. Good pussy. Good pussy," I keep repeating.

"What you say?" she asks.

"Nothing, but like I was saying before you interrupted me. Keep talking shit in front of your lonely ass, miserable friends and Imma embarrass you," I tell her.

"Who he talkin' about?"

"I know he didn't."

"Getcha man in check, Keisha!" her friends hollered in the background. I know she has me on speakerphone, but I don't care.

"Fuck you, Marques! You think 'cause you throw a couple dollars at a bitch, that you the shit and can do what you want. I'm not the one to be played with!" she screams and hangs up the phone.

I ask the waitress for my bill. Keisha knows better, but she wants to show off for her 'friends', so after paying the waitress for my food, I hightail it straight to Druid Hill Avenue. Just like I thought, Keisha and her hoodrat committee are sitting on a bench, hee-heeing and talking louder than necessary. She spots my car and looks like a deer caught in headlights.

"Yeah, bitch, you know what time it is," I say to myself. I get out my car and march straight towards her. All of a sudden everyone gets quiet. "Bitch, I told you to stop talking shit and showing off for these hoes!" I yell and slap her across the face. None of her so-called friends say anything or jump up to help her. "You stupid as fuck! Putting on a show for the same bitches that been tryin' to get at me behind your back. You giving them exactly what they want, for me to leave your dumbass alone!" I yell and point in her face. All her friends start talking shit and denying my accusations.

I smile because I know the real deal. "Monique, you sucked my dick in a stairwell two weeks ago for a gram of powder. Cashmere, bitch, I got naked pictures that you sent to my phone. Demetria, I don't want you. You gave one of my niggas the monster. You ain't nothing but a walking death sentence, bitch. Denise, I ain't had you yet. You can definitely get the 'D' anytime you want with your fine ass."

I laugh at all of the stunned looks on everyone's face. Keisha turns around and punches Monique in the face, then lunged at Cashmere. Three of them start beating on each other savagely. I wink at Denise and she winks back, so I walk up to her and tell her to put her number in my phone.

"I'll call you soon," I tell her and begin to walk off.

Halfway to my car, I can hear Keisha yelling for me, "Please Marques. I'm sorry. I won't do it again, I promise!" She grabs my shirt, trying to hug on me.

"Bitch, get off me! I warned you and you kept bumping your gums." I push her off of me and she falls flat on her ass. A group of niggas that are standing close by start laughing. Keisha sits on the ground, crying, and ashamed.

"I'm done wit her. If any of y'all want that, feel free. She's a straight freak yo!," I tell them. "You said fuck me, but it's fuck you bitch. You played yourself," I tell her and get in my car. I go through the contacts on my phone to see who I'm going to spend my Saturday with.

Bernadette—I haven't seen her in a hot minute.

"Hello?" a soft voice answers the phone.

"You got time for me, ma?" I ask.

"I always have time for you, baby. Come on over and I'll cook you a hot meal."

She doesn't have to tell me twice. I pull out the parking space and head towards I-95. Bernadette is a county girl that knows how to treat a man. She cooks, cleans, keeps herself up, and stays to herself. She and I have been on and off ever since we were teenagers. If I wasn't with Sonya, I was with Bernadette. After moving away from Harford County and into the city, I became so busy with business. I could move her to Bmore, but I'd rather she stay in the County. As long as she remains my best-kept secret, she'll be safe from my bullshit and the drama that comes with my 'job'. While driving down 95, Keisha calls me; I send her ass to voicemail and focus on the highway. Forty minutes later, I arrive in Aberdeen. I call Bernadette to let her know that I'm in town.

"Okay. See you in a few," she says and hangs up.

When I see the big blue water tower, I know that I'm close to her house. I turn into Brentwood Townhomes, and then take a right onto Custis Street. Bernadette's car is parked in front of a townhouse on the left, so I parallel park behind her. As I'm exiting my car, she comes running out the door and down the steps.

"What's good, love?" I smile as she jumps in my arms. The smell of vanilla invades my nose. "Damn, you smell good."

"Come on in; the food is almost done," she says and leads me into the house.

The aroma of some type of Italian dish and the smooth 90's R&B jams playing softly in the background makes me feel at home. The pitter-patter of little feet coming down the stairs catches my attention. "Hey, little man, what's up?" I ask him as I pick him up.

"Where you been?" he asks, "My momma said she misses you."

"Marques Demetrius Brown Junior, didn't I tell you to wash your hands and get ready for dinner?" Bernadette yells from the kitchen.

"Go on and do what your mom told you to do," I tell him as I put him back down.

"Okay, daddy. I'll be right back. Don't go anywhere, okay?" he says.

"I promise I'll be here, son."

CHAPTER 13

Sonya

It was good to hear Toya's voice this morning. When we hung up with each other, I took a shower and got dressed. Marques was already gone when I woke up, so I call him but he doesn't answer. Come to think about it, he didn't come home last night. I notice that his side of the bed hasn't been slept in. Before leaving my condo, I take one last look in my full-length mirror. My Joana splatter paint skinny jeans show off my curves. The shirt I have on doesn't seem right, so I take it off.

As I go through my closet, I spot the perfect top for my ensemble, an emerald green Kaftan Caftan blouse. To top off my outfit, I accessorized with a Lariat white gold and pearl necklace, fourteen-carat white gold, emerald and diamond bracelet and some eighteen-carat white gold, emerald and pearl earrings. Satisfied with my look, I slip on a pair of silver glitter Jimmy Choo degrade point toe stilettos. Hmm, I'm missing something. My silver Salvator Ferragamo Miss Vera clutch and my Chanel shades. Now, I'm feeling myself and posing in the mirror.

"Never leave the house half stepping," I say to myself as I walk out the door.

Thank God Marques drove the Honda, because I hate driving that thing. After applying my lip gloss, I blast Beyoncé's "Partition" and head to a cafe on Aliceanna Street in Fells Point to grab a bite to eat. While looking over the menu, I notice a fine dark chocolate man glancing at me. I take off my Chanel shades and place them on the table so that he can get a good look at my face.

"Are you ready to place your order, ma'am?" the waitress says as she steps in the way of viewing Mr. Chocolate.

"Um, yes. I'll have the scrambled eggs without the yolk, toast, and two strips of turkey bacon, please." I smile and hand her the menu.

The waitress walks off to place my order, but Mr. Chocolate is not in his seat. I look out the window to see if I can spot him getting into his car. There he is, standing next to a black Cadillac CTS, talking on his phone. After hanging up, he comes back in and returns to his seat. Something about him gives me Goosebumps.

"Here's your breakfast; egg whites, toast and turkey bacon. Is there anything else I can get you?" the waitress asks.

"No, thank you, but I would like to pay for it now," I tell her.

"Your meal has already been paid for by that gentleman over there," the waitress says and points at Mr. Chocolate.

"Okay, thank you. That'll be all," I say surprised and flattered at the kind gesture from Mr. Chocolate. While enjoying my light breakfast, he gets up from his seat and hands the waitress a tip.

Instead of walking out the door, he walks up to me. "Excuse me, Queen, do you mind if I keep you company?"

You can do a lot more to me, I think to myself.

"Sure, have a seat Mr..." I wait for him to tell me his name.

"Mr. Wettles, but you can call me Angelo." He kisses the back of my hand and smiles. Lord, he has dimples and a flawless smile. He licked his lips and I instantly cream myself.

"I'm Sonya. It's a pleasure to meet you, Angelo. He and I sit and talk for what seems like only thirty minutes, but turns out to be a couple of hours. He seems to be very smart, definitely funny, well mannered, and oh, so fine.

I glance at my watch and realize that too much time has passed. "I better go, I have a lot to do today," I tell him.

"I'll walk you to your car," he says and holds out his hand to help me out of my seat. On the way out, Angelo holds the door open for me.

"So, I enjoyed our talk," I tell him as we approach the Benz.

"Yeah, me too. How about we do it again?" Angelo says.

I reach into my clutch to get a pen and piece of paper. "This is my cell phone number. I'll be expecting a call." I hand him the phone number.

"You can count on it." He smiles. There go those dimples again. I get in my car and he closes the door for me, "It was nice meeting you, Sonya." He bites his lip and steps back.

I honk my horn and pull off, hoping that Mr. Wettles and I cross paths again. Putting Angelo to the back of my mind and getting straight to business, I speed dial Trey.

"What's good ma?" he answers.

"I'm just checking in with you. Did Beast and Sincere make it there yet?" I ask. "Nah, not yet. I told them where to meet me, because we had to change spots," he answers. "Speaking of the spot, how did the relocation work out?" "Same area, new building. It wasn't hard for our clientele to find us," Trey answers. "Alright I'll call you later. I'm heading to our new strip club on East Baltimore," I tell him.

"Oh word? Y'all bought that strip joint from the Arab?" Trey asks.

"We gave him an offer he couldn't refuse." I laugh.

"That's what's up! Aight, back to business. Bye." Trey hangs up.

While parking my car, I notice a dark tinted Crown Vic driving out of the parking lot. "What's up, Bull?" I greet the bouncer at the door.

"Shit, I can't call it," he replies.

"Is that all you say?" I ask him as I walk in. Bull doesn't say anything, just holds the door open for me. The smell of pork is in the air. Damn, cops already fucking with us. "Hey, Truck. What's going on?" I ask.

"Five-O came in here asking about Ahmed. Supposedly him and his wife skipped town after chopping up their kids. They think it may be an honor killing," he tells me.

Time to put on an award-winning act, I think to myself. "Say what? What kind of monster would kill innocent children? That's fucked up," I say with shock.

"You don't have to put on an act for me. I know the real deal, ma. Save that performance for five-O. I think he deserved everything he got. You don't have to worry about me saying shit," Truck says.

As I look around the strip club, I realize that Marques and I didn't get rid of the surveillance footage. Fuck!

***

Clyde

Mookie thinks he's slick, smiling all up in Toya's face. He has no idea that he's playing with fire and Toya is the devil. She is not to be toyed with or underestimated. I'm surprised she didn't go off the deep end when she found out about Michelle.

Toya comes into my office and sits down.

"You seem distracted. Care to share?" she asks.

I sit down and lean back in my chair. "Mookie just came to me 'bout a business proposition."

Toya sits up, giving me her full attention.

"He knows someone in Fort Worth dat want ta do a trade," I tell her.

"What kind of trade?" Toya asks.

I take a deep a breath. "Some green for some pills like Percs, Xanax, roxies, and syrup. They pretty much got everything."

Toya stands up and paces my office. "What did you tell him?"

"I told him dat I would have ta check wit my connect and get back to him. He don't know it's you," I tell her.

She walks to the window and stares out. "Do you trust him with that much weight? 'Cause if he fucks up, I'll blame you," Toya says with a deadly look in her eyes.

I get deep in thought, wondering if I should put my neck on the line. Mookie is a sneaky nigga, but we've been friends since elementary.

"Personally, I think you need to think really hard. I don't trust him, but that's your friend. You know him better than I do," she says.

"I trust him when it comes to business, but not when it comes to you." I laugh.

"Okay, so we're going through with it?" Toya asks.

I nod my head in agreement. "I'm gonna call Michelle to see if she wanna go wit' us to the club tonight," I tell Toya to see her reaction.

She smiles at me, "Sure, baby. That's a great way to break the ice. Good idea." Toya leaves my office to give me some privacy.

"Hey, bae, you miss me?" Michelle answers the phone. "I wanna run something by you real quick. Don't say nothing; just listen to what I have to say. Toya knows about us, don't ask how. She not trippin' though, but she want me to share you wit' her," I explain.

Michelle is quiet for a moment as if she's considering it. "I'm willin' ta give it uh try, I guess."

"Good, cause we goin' out tonight and want you to come wit' us, so you and Toya can get better acquainted. Ya down?" I ask her.

"Yeah, I'll be ready by ten. We goin' ta Bunkie?" she asks.

"Most likely. We'll be at your apartment around ten, maybe sooner. Make sure you ready." Michelle and I hang up with each other and I jump out my seat excited that I'm getting every man's fantasy served on a silver platter by none other than my main bitch, Toya.

"Bae!" I call Toya as I walk to the kitchen for a drink. She doesn't answer, so I look for her in our room.When I get to the room, I see Toya sitting on the edge of the bed in a daze. I watch her for a few minutes to see what she does, but she doesn't move a single muscle or blink.I wonder what she's thinking about. "Bae! Earth to Toya!"

No response, she just sits there. I walk up to her and kiss her forehead. She looks up at me blankly, then finally blinks twenty seconds later. "You say something, boo?" she asks.

I sit next to her and put my arm around her, while telling her about me and Michelle's conversation. Toya smiles, "I'm glad she's willing to be open with us. I can't wait."

I look deep into Toya's eyes and ask, "What were you thinking about a few minutes ago?" She shakes her head and says, "Nothing special, just daydreaming."

I leave the issue alone, pat her on the leg and go to my closet. I want to look good tonight, so I go through my clothes to see what I can put together. I pull out my black Stefano Ricci jeans and red Salvatore Ferragamo polo shirt and show them to Toya.

"What you think bae?" I ask her.

She nods her head in approval. "You should wear those red and black North Face boots with it," she suggests.

"You right, it does match up," I admit.

Now that I have my outfit put together, it's time for a fresh cut and line up. I call my barber, Wayne. "Wut it dew?" he answers.

"I need you to make uh house call fa me. There's uh big tip in it fa you."

"Be there when I get done wit' dis head, bo," Wayne says.

"Dat's what's up, I'll be here," I tell him and hang up. Toya walks up behind me and runs her hand from my chest all the way down to my belt buckle. "Hold on, bae. I'm still wore out from last night," I tell her. "Who said anything about fucking and who told you that you could talk?" she purrs. I kiss her and lick on her neck. Toya pushes my face away and gets on her knees.

CHAPTER 14

Toya

It doesn't surprise me that Clyde would approach me about a business deal with Mookie. To be honest, I know that nigga is up to no good. What does bother me is that Clyde is willing to put his neck on the line for his no good friend. I don't want to kill Clyde if Mookie fucks up, but I will. My motto is and will always be: money over niggas, regardless of how I feel about him. Love don't pay the bills and business is business, period.

After leaving Clyde in his office to call Michelle, I went in the room to wait for him. As I sit there, my mind takes me back to the winter of 2009. My car was snowed in, so Sonya and I couldn't get back to the city.

"Girl, I told you we shouldn't have stayed the night down here," Sonya complained.

She and I had come to Harford County to meet up with my boyfriend Tek and his friend Marques. Tek and I had been dating for a little over a year; I was so in love with him. He spoiled me rotten, and whatever I wanted, he got it.

"Shut up, Sonya. You weren't doing all the complaining last night while Marques was digging them guts out." I laughed. Sonya gave me the middle finger and stuck out her tongue. "Save all the tongue action for Marques," I teased. After throwing a few snowballs at each other, Sonya and I decided to head back into Tek's apartment.

"Our car is snowed in, thanks to this damn blizzard," I tell Tek as we walk back in.   Sonya sat in Marques's lap. "Yeah and now we're stuck here," she whined.

For the next two hours, all four of us munched on popcorn and watched a movie. Tek looks at his watch and stands up. "I gotta go handle something in Church Green," he tells Marques.

"You need me to go with you?" Marques asked.

"Nuh, I'm good. It'll only take me a sec. What y'all wanna eat yo?" We debated on what to eat and decided on cheese steaks. "Well, I was talking about going to get snacks from Sid's. It'll take a hot minute to get the cheese steaks 'cause of the snow. I'll be back by here before I go get the food," Tek says.

He goes to his room and comes out with a duffle bag, then walks out the door. I hear his car start outside followed by some arguing. Sonya and I run to the window to see what's going on. Tek was in a heated argument with some female that looked like she was pregnant. So I lace up my Timberlands and head outside with Sonya close behind.

"Why the fuck are you all up in his face? What's going on, Tek?" I inquire.

Tek looks at me and that's when the bitch decided to pounce on him, cursing and hitting. Another girl gets out of a car; I'm assuming that it must be her friend. Sonya already knows what's up and posts up beside me. I grab the girl that is hitting on Tek and began to use her face as a punching bag. Sonya delivers a two-piece to her friend for trying to jump me. Tek tries to pull me off of the girl, but I wasn't having it. I threw her to the icy sidewalk and began to stomp on her. The final kick landed on her head, causing it to bounce off the ground. I rock-a-byed her ass to sleep; the bitch went night night.

Sonya was still doing her thing with the other girl, screaming all kinds of profanities and words that don't even exist. Tek pulls me away. "She had enough. You and Sonya need to go back into the apartment and stay there."

Not satisfied with the damage I had already done, I snatched away from Tek and charged towards the girl that Sonya was whooping on. I reached into my coat pocket and pulled out a box cutter. I pushed Sonya off of the girl. "I got this Sonya, move!"

I straddled the girl and opened the box cutter, smiling like the Cheshire cat. The girl's eyes became wide with fear, causing my nipples to get hard and my pussy to pulsate. The thought of using her face as an Etch A Sketch turned me on. "You tried to jump in? You thought you was gonna jump me, bitch?" I screamed.

I flashed out; I can't recall what I had done. When I came to, my hands, coat, jeans and face were splattered with blood. The bitch was still alive, but the damage to her face would make her wish I had killed her. Sonya dragged me back into the apartment as Tek jumped into his car and drove off.

"Dammit Toya! The hell was all that? I had it under control!" Sonya yelled.

She led me to the bathroom and began to remove my coat. She shakes her head and sucks her teeth. I didn't realize that I still had the box cutter gripped in my hand. Sonya pries the blade from me and continues to strip me naked.

"Take a shower. Get all this shit off of you." She turns on the water and helps me into the tub. "I'll be right back with some clothes," she said.

I laughed because she was frantic and the visions of what I had done to those girls were hilarious. When I finally stopped laughing, I noticed Sonya standing in the bathroom with my clothes, staring at me like I'm some kind of lunatic.

"What's wrong with you? You look like you seen a ghost." I smile.

"Bitch, you crazy as hell." She laughs. Sonya and I laughed ourselves to tears, feeding off of each other's laughter.

After getting cleaned up and dressed, we joined Marques in the living room. "You straight, ma?" he asked.

"I'm more than straight," I replied.

"Good. You lucky we're in Washington Park, yo," Marques said.

"What's that suppose to mean?" Sonya asked.

"It means you don't have to worry about anyone around here calling 5-0. Still need to get y'all to a hotel, 'cause if those broads go to the hospital and I'm pretty sure they will, the hospital will notify the police. I got a plan though, no worries," he said.

When Tek arrived back at the apartment, he rushed to his room with a different duffle bag than what he had left with. My curiosity was piqued. "What were those duffle bags for?" I asked him.

"Damn, girl, you're nosey," Sonya said.

"Sonya..." I give her a look that shuts her up.

"The less you know, the better off you'll be," Tek replied.

"Haven't I shown you that I can handle myself?" I was offended.

"You showed him that your ass is crazy." Sonya laughed.

"Sonya, why you testing my patience? If you were somebody else, I would have fucked you up the first time you butt into my conversation," I said to her.

Sonya turned her attention back to the television and I focused back on Tek.

"Maybe one day, but I don't think you're ready yet." Tek kissed me on the forehead and began to walk towards the door.

"Hold up, Tek. I gotta run something by you," Marques said. Tek turned around and gave Marques his full attention. "Take the girls with you to get the food and drop them off at a hotel. By the time you get back, I'll have their car shoveled out and we can meet them back at the room. That way, if the police come today, the girls won't be here. Tomorrow they'll be able to head back to the city."

"Good idea. Y'all go get your stuff so we can go," Tek said.

Tek followed me to his room to help me gather the things that I had brought in my overnight bag. In the process of packing, I came across the bloody clothes.

"Come here, boo," I beckon Tek.

"What's up?" he asked.

Without saying a word, I began to remove my pants and panties. He smiled. "Baby, we don't have time for all that right now."

I unbuckled his belt, unbuttoned and unzipped his pants, and pulled down his boxers. "Looks like you're not in a rush to leave," I said.

Tek knelt down and licked on my pearl like a pro; I came quickly. He pushed me into the wall and fucked me wildly as we stood there. "Is that what you want? Want me murder that pussy?" he asked.

I screamed, scratched, bit, pulled my hair, and cursed. I didn't care how much noise I made; Tek pummeled my pussy just the way I liked it. After gaining our composure, Tek and I came out the room with my things. Sonya knew she was on thin ice with me, so she kept her mouth shut. Marques sat on the couch laughing at us.

"Fuck you, Marques." I laughed.

By the time we left the apartment, it was dark outside and it had finally stopped snowing. Tek opened the car door for me to get in and shut it after I was seated. Who said thugs don't have manners? I watch him in admiration as he wipes the snow off of the windows. There was nothing that I wouldn't do for him. He and I could have had something really special, but he changed all that.

***

Trey

I was at the Woodlawn location for about two hours before Beast and Sincere arrived. We gave each other dap and got down to business. "Let me see what we're working with," I say as I zip open the first duffle bag.

"That's straight up gas, yo," Sincere brags.

I nod in agreement; the weed was definitely potent. I check the second duffle bag and ask Beast if it's the same product as last time. "Black tar heroin, same shit. That boy will put a fiend on his ass," Beast answers.

"That's what's up. Here's what I owe. You're welcome to count it here if you need to," I tell them.

"That won't be necessary. Toya always does good business," Beast says.

"Aight, son. Well, I'll see y'all soon," I tell them.

Before walking out the door, Sincere turns around. "One more thing before I leave. Word back home is that there's a price on Toya's head and anybody associated with her. Watch ya back, son."

"Good lookin' out, yo. I'll make sure to look into that." Before going home to prepare for my second job, I make sure to call the other spots to warn them about the potential threat and to keep an eye out for trouble. I take one last look around then head home to prepare for work.

Someone is out for my sister, but who? She has killed and hurt so many people that it's hard to pinpoint who has a hit on her and why. While driving home, I listen to 92Q Jams, attempting to drown out my thoughts. Something makes the hairs on the back of my neck stand up when I get home; somebody is here. My door isn't locked; I never leave my condo unlocked. On full alert, I pull out my glock and put one in the chamber. Slowly walking in, I spot the silhouette of someone sitting on my sofa.

"You can put your piece down. If I wanted you dead, you'd be crab food by now," he says.

I flick on the light to see a dark skinned nigga smiling at me. "Please, have a seat, Trey."

"Who are you and what the fuck are you doing in my shit?" I ask him.

"How rude of me. I didn't introduce myself." He stands up and walks over to me with his hand out for a handshake. I dismiss his gesture and look at him, waiting for an answer. He smiles again and walks to my bar to help himself to some Crown.

"My name is Angelo, no last name needed. From my understanding, your sister has something that belongs to me and I'm here to get what is mine," he says. This nigga must be crazy or just plain stupid to be all up in my shit, confronting me about my sister. Angelo laughs. "You seem lost. I know you're probably wondering what I'm talking about. Am I right?"

I continue to stare at him. "Get to the point on why you're here, so you can be on your way, nigga."

He nods his head. "Years ago I was running an empire. MY empire, that took a lot of blood, sweat, and tears to build. The blood of many victims, my sweat, and the tears of many grief stricken mothers that had to bury those of whom I had to sacrifice for the benefit of MY empire. Unfortunately, I got pinched and had to do some numbers. Before going on my little 'vacation', I temporarily handed my crown to my brother. Are you following where I'm going with this?" he asks.

"Cut to the damn chase," I bark at him.

Angelo smiles and continues his story. "My brother held shit down for me, a natural born hustla. Along the way he fucked up. He had one weakness that he couldn't deny. Take a wild guess on who it was."

I don't answer him, but I have a good idea on who he may be referring to.

"Your sister, Toya. That bitch is as cold blooded as they come. I can't lie, she is a natural born killer. I could have used her expertise, but she fucked up when she killed the only family I had left."

"What the fuck you tryin' to say? You want a war?" I ask.

"It doesn't have to come to that. I'm a reasonable person. I'm willing to have a sit down with your sister to negotiate," Angelo says.

"If you want to meet with Toya, it's not going to happen. Everything goes through me and my girl Sonya first. Toya will decide from there if you're worth talking to," I reply.

"Sweet, sweet Sonya. I can dig it." He grabs his crotch. "Here's my number. I expect to receive a call within twenty-four hours to let me know when and where you want to meet up."

Angelo hands me a card and walks out. What the fuck just happened? Without time to waste on what just occurred, I get dressed for work and hurry to my work vehicle. On the way to East Fayette Street, I couldn't shake the feeling that shit was about to get real in the streets of Baltimore. One thing I know for sure is that Sonya and Toya are off limits. I'll die before I let a muthafucka harm them. Before walking into the building, I clear my mind and get into work mode.

"Hey, Detective Cummings. How was your weekend?" Detective Hayes asks me.

CHAPTER 15

Marques

Bernadette spoiled me rotten last night. I woke up to the smell of turkey bacon, eggs, biscuits, pancakes, and grits. As we eat Sunday breakfast together as a family, I realize what I'm missing out on. I mean, do I really want to continue running the streets? I have some serious thinking to do about my life and where I'm headed if I stay in these streets. After enjoying our meal, I helped Bernadette clean the kitchen and wash the dishes.

"I been thinking about making this permanent. I'm ready to chill out and be a family," I tell her.

Bernadette stops washing the dishes and faces me. "So what are you trying to say?"

I grab her by the hand and lead her to the dining room table to sit down. Sitting in front of her with both of her hands in mine, I look deep into her eyes. "I'm ready to be exclusive. I want to move back here to Harford County for us to be a family. I'm tired and there's only two places I'm headed if I keep running those streets, dead or in prison."

Bernadette begins to cry uncontrollably.

"What's wrong, baby? Did I say something wrong?" I ask her.

It takes her a few moments to get her emotions under control. "Nothing is wrong, boo. These are tears of joy. You have no idea how long I've waited to hear those words."

She hugs me and kisses me passionately. Deep down I know that I made the right choice. M.J. comes down the stairs and looks at us with a confused looked on his face. "What's wrong, Mommy?"

"Nothing's wrong, son. For once, everything is right," she tells him.

I scoop him into my arms. "Let's go find something to put on, so we can get out this house."

M.J. giggles. "Where are we going, Daddy?"

"Somewhere fun. You have any ideas?" I ask him.

"Um, the park?" he asks.

"Aight, we'll go to the park in Havre De Grace," I tell him.

Bernadette, M.J., and I spent the whole day together. I can definitely see me doing this everyday. Later on we went to evening church to receive the word. "Mr. Brown! How ya doing brotha? We haven't seen you in awhile," Pastor Williams says.

We shake hands. "Yeah, it has been awhile. I've been staying in the city," I explain.

"Yes! Yes! Bernadette did mention that to me. Enjoy the service," he says.

Service begins shortly after taking our seats in the pew.

"Good evening, brothas and sistas. Today, I wanna talk about forgiveness. How many of you find it hard to forgive those that have wronged you? Do you let it fester, grow inside of you, eat you alive, and consume your soul?" The pastor looks around the church. "I see I touched some of you. Well, tell me something..." He looks around the church again. "How many of you would sacrifice your only child for the forgiveness of EVERYONE? How many of you paid the ultimate sacrifice? I don't think y'all hear me! In order to receive God's forgiveness, we must forgive those who harm us." Pastor Williams wipes the sweat from his brow.

"Amen!" People shout throughout the church. The sermon was over an hour and a half later.

"I really enjoyed that," Bernadette says.

"Yeah, Pastor Williams sure knows how to break it down to you," I reply.

The pastor really touched a sore spot with me. I've done so much dirt, killed, lied, and cheated. I just hope that God forgives me for all the wrong I've done. There's just one last thing I have to get done before I let it all go. Tomorrow I will go on Edmund Street to make one final withdraw at one of the stash houses.

For dinner, I took my family to The Promenade Grille in Havre De Grace to eat. Afterwards, we went home to get M.J. ready for school the next morning. "Daddy, are you going to be here when I get home tomorrow?" M.J. asks as he splashes in the tub.

"I'll be here. I'll come get you from the bus stop," I tell him.

"You promise?" he asks.

"I promise. I'm not going anywhere. I'll be here everyday from now on."

***

Sonya

I spent my Saturday deleting all of the surveillance footage and cleaning out Ahmed's office. Luckily, the bartender was smart enough to tell the police to come back with a warrant if they need to search the property. When I finished covering our tracks, I held a meeting with all of the employees.

"Starting today, all of you will be under new management. Ahmed signed over ownership of this club to Ms. Cummings. I will be in charge until further notice. You can expect pay raises and the dancers will keep a bigger percentage of their earnings. Any questions?"

One of the dancers raises her hand. "Hi, I'm Sapphire and I just wanna know what happened wit' Ahmed."

"Truck, do you mind explaining to Sapphire what's going on?" I ask.

Truck walks to the front of the room. "Some detectives came by asking questions. Apparently, Ahmed and his wife disappeared shortly after signing over ownership of the club. We're assuming that they are the ones that killed their two children, signed over the club, and ran back to Saudi Arabia," Truck explained.

"Thank you, Truck. If by chance the police return with more questions, please send them to your assistant manager Joy, Truck, or Ginger. Meeting is over. Everyone back to work, and for those of you who came in on their day off, you are free to leave."

As everyone walked out, they shook my hand and expressed how happy they were about Ahmed being gone. I make it home at eleven in the evening, but Marques isn't there. There's no sign of him even coming home today. I try calling him, but still no answer. Before going to bed, I fill my jacuzzi tub with hot water and scented lavender oil to soak away the stress of the day. As my tub fills, I pour myself a glass of Moscato and put Sade on my surround sound.

I light my vanilla bean candles around my tub and strip naked. While soaking in lavender heaven, jamming to Sweetest Taboo, my phone rings. I try to ignore the ringing and enjoy my bath but answer after the third ring. "Hello?"

"Hey, Gorgeous. You know who this is?" a guy's voice comes over the phone and instantly my nipples get hard.

"Hmmm. I think I do. Your voice sounds familiar. Could it be...Angelo?"

He chuckles. "You think you know me huh?" he asks.

"Not saying I know you, but I know that voice from anywhere," I flirt.

"Is that right? You at home? I can hear some Sade playin' in the background."

"Umhmm. Preparing for bed. It's been a long day," I reply.

"Sounds like you're in the tub. I can hear water as well. You need some company? I'm a good back rubber," he jokes.

"Nuh. Not tonight, but I'm free tomorrow for lunch."

Angelo gets quiet for a few seconds. "I guess I can move around some things on my schedule to make time for you. What do you suggest?" Angelo asks.

"I'll be in Park Heights around noon. So we can meet up at West Indian Flavour around one. That's fine with you?"

"Sounds like a plan. I'll be there," he says.

"Alright, Mr. Wettles. It was nice hearing from you. Sweet dreams."

"Goodnight, Queen. Don't dream too hard about me. You might soak your panties." He laughed and hung up.

Angelo's voice gives me Goosebumps and little does he know, I was wet the moment he spoke. I couldn't help rubbing on my clit and bringing myself to an orgasm as I thought about all the things I wanted to do to him. After my bath, I walk around naked to air dry, preparing for the next day.

I pick out a white Boho Chiffon mini dress and a pair of Jimmy Choo rose and crystal embellished satin T-strap sandals. Then I go further into my walk in closet and open the wall containing all of my sunglasses. Behind the wall is my secret compartment of guns. I choose my all white custom-made desert eagle and put it in a white leather Jimmy Choo Riki handbag. Fly and lethal, exactly what I was going for.

CHAPTER 16

Toya

"You say something, boo?" I ask Clyde.

I don't know how long I was zoned out. That flashback caught me off guard. Clyde seemed a little worried about me, but I put his mind at ease with some exquisite head. After helping him pick out his outfit for the night and relaxing his mind, I figured that I might as well get my things ready too. I want to match Clyde, so I choose a red, exotic lace V-cut mini dress and some black fuck me stilettos.

"I like dat right there. Imma have to fight niggas off you." Clyde smiles.

It took me an hour to get my hair right. I prefer my natural beauty over make up, so I just put on some red lip stick and gloss. Shortly after getting dolled up, there is a knock at the door. Clyde answers and greets whoever came by. It must be his barber, so I go to the living room to meet him.

"Wayne, dis my guh Toya. Toya dis is my nigga Wayne," Clyde introduces us.

"Nice to meet you Wayne," I hold out my hand for a handshake but he kisses the back of my hand instead.

"The pleasure's all mine. Clyde, where you been hiding dis beauty? She speaks all proper too; you must be from New York." Wayne laughs.

"Hey, hey! Getcho own, bruh! This one is mines and off limits. She from Baltimore though." Clyde play boxes Wayne.

I give the men some privacy and go to my room. While watching the news, the story about the lawyer I killed is airing.

They still don't have any leads. I'm not surprised; they'll never solve that case. I'm a professional at everything I do. The lawyer's wife pleads on TV. for anyone with information to please come forward.

"Boo hoo, bitch! If only you knew that your hubby died for this pussy." I laugh.

I turn the TV off the moment they begin to talk about Trump. Around nine, Clyde and I get dressed and are out the door by nine thirty. We pull up at Chateau Deville and walk to Michelle's apartment. From the looks of her place, I can see that Clyde must give her crumbs. Her furniture is mediocre and the apartment is too small for my liking.

"I'm almost finished getting ready. Y'all have uh seat," Michelle says and goes back into her room. Within thirty minutes she's ready to go. She needed an extra thirty minutes for that? She had on some Levis, a blue cut off shirt and a knock off Gucci purse. I could tell she had on a wig and she had the nerve to put on flip-flops. I kinda feel sorry for the girl. I mean, who wears flip-flops to a club?

The three of us arrive at the club in Bunkie around eleven thirty. It's much smaller than I'm used to, but what do you expect in the country? On the way in, Clyde was greeted by a lot of people, males and females. I caught the eyes of a few of his 'friends' and some smirks from a lot of bitches. I really don't mind the hate, it just means that I'm 'that bitch'. These niggas are so thirsty, either trying to grab my hand or stare at my ass.

Michelle notices all of the attention I'm getting and tries to play it off like it doesn't bother her, but I can see that green eyed monster—envy—peeking its head out. "Yall find uh spot and I'll get some drinks," Clyde says.

"We 'bout to hit the dance floor," Michelle replies.

She grabs me by the hand and leads me to the floor. Without any hesitation, Michelle starts feeling me up and down and grinding on me. This stops a lot of niggas in their tracks to admire the freak show Michelle is putting on. After two songs, we joined Clyde at the bar. His back was facing the bar, watching us, as he talked to a heavy set, dark skinned guy. Both of them were smiling from ear to ear, obviously happy about Michelle's little show.

"Rob Rob, dis my guh Toya I was tellin' you 'bout. You already know Michelle," Clyde introduces.

"Hey Rob Rob, how you been? Long time, no see," Michelle greets him.

As she goes in to hug Rob Rob, he steps right past her and greeted me. "What it do, Toya? I heard a lot of good things 'bout you. We got some business to discuss later," he says and kisses my hand.

Michelle crosses her arms in frustration over how Rob Rob had disregarded her. "I'm sure we do. How about you come by tomorrow and we can talk," I tell him.

"Dat's what's up. Aight, bo, I'm bout to head out. Good lookin' out cuz," Rob Rob says and gives Clyde dap. Okay, that was one, now I want to meet the rest of the shot callers this town has to offer. Rob Rob will be number one on my list of 'shit to do'.

***

Clyde

I must admit, I was the man tonight. Toya had all the niggas drooling at the mouth, including some bitches. On the way home, I stopped by a friend's house behind the coliseum to get some E pills. Tonight my fantasy was finally coming true. Afterwards, I made a pit stop at one of the Arab stores to get some condoms, bottles of water, gum, Vaseline, inhalers, and a bootleg porn flick. As we head to the house, I give Toya and Michelle a pill and take one for myself. Michelle downs hers but Toya hands me hers back.

"You know I don't take drugs, I sell them," she says.

By the time we get to the house, the pill is taking its effect. I lead both girls to the bathroom and begin to undress Michelle and put her in the shower. Then I undress Toya nice and slow and place one of her legs on top of the toilet seat. As Michelle washed up, I ate Toya's pussy until she creamed into my mouth, then placed her into the shower with Michelle. They begin to wash each other; the sight of the soapy suds cascading down their bodies turns me on.

I take off my clothes with the speed of lightning and stroke my dick at the sight of two women in the shower together. I can feel the urge to cum so I step up to the tub. "I'm bouta cum."
Toya pushes Michelle's head down to catch the load in her mouth. "Ugh! Shit! Yeah, swallow all dat shit," I growl.

Toya and Michelle get out of the shower and head into the bedroom as I take a quick shower. When I walk into the room, Toya riding Michelle's face greets me. Toya's playing with her nipples and staring at me as she bites her lip. Instead of joining in, I sit down and watch them go to work as I stroke myself.

"That's it, bitch. Eat that pussy like your life depends on it," Toya says. She's still staring at me, but something in her eyes shifted. "Uh, fuck! I'm cumming!"

Toya rides Michelle's face harder. Michelle starts to squirm and flail her arms as if she's fighting for air. Damn, I should have known she was gonna try some crazy shit. Toya climbs off of Michelle's face and laughs. "Are you okay?"

"You trying to kill me? I couldn't breath!" Michelles yells.

Toya grabs Michelle by the throat. "Stop all the bitch ass crying. Come here, Clyde."

I stand up and walk towards the bed. Toya puts her hand around the back of Michelle's neck while her other hand is still wrapped around the front of her neck, choking the shit out of her. Michelle's mouth is wide open, gasping for air.

"Fuck her mouth," Toya orders me. I'm kind of scared of the monster that Toya was becoming right before my eyes. The look she gives me is devilish and I do as I'm told. I begin to fuck Michelle's mouth mercilessly; Toya occasionally lets Michelle get some air. I start to get turned on by the brutal sexcapade. Toya can see the look on my face and smiles up at me.

"Cum in this bitch's hair."

After a few more strokes, I pull out and cum all over the top of Michelle's head. Toya lets go of her throat and falls back laughing. Michelle rubs her neck and coughs violently. As she fights for air and oxygen, I climb on top of Toya and begin to fuck her brains out.

"Harder!" she screams.

I pump has hard as I can, but it doesn't seem to bother her. Toya rolls her eyes and forces me onto my back. I have never been man handled in the bed before, but it turns me on. She rides me as she squeezes my neck with both hands. I don't know if she's trying to kill me or if this is some kind of sick game to her. Surprisingly, I came harder than I ever have in my life. I mean, I was seeing stars and shit.

Toya climbs back onto Michelle's face and tells me to fuck her from the back. She's going crazy; the sensation of getting her pussy licked and penetrated has her cumming back to back. When she's had enough, Toya climbs off of Michelle and slaps her across the face.

"Da fuck you slap me for?" Michelle screams.

Toya ignores her and heads towards the bathroom to wash up. While Toya does her thing, I wrap up with a condom and proceed to fuck Michelle. She's loving it, screaming, and her eyes are rolling to the back of her head. I look up at the ceiling, focused on not cumming too soon when all of a sudden, I feel Michelle squirting. Wait...Michelle is not a squirter. I look down and there is Toya smiling at me with a bloody knife in her hand. Michelle wasn't squirting, that was blood. Toya had gutted her while I was fucking her. I didn't hear her enter back into the room. Michelle is cut open from the neck down to her naval.

"What the fuck?! What did you do Toya? Why?" She doesn't say anything; instead she pulls off my condom and pushes me back onto the bed. Toya tries to give me head, but the sight of all that blood and Michelle's insides, turned me off. Toya gets up and puts the knife to my neck.

"If you EVER fuck around on me again, I'll kill you! Then I'm killing everyone you love. You really thought I was okay with you fucking with another bitch? How stupid do you think I am? Don't insult my muthafuckin' intelligence," she whispers in my ear as if someone else can hear.

Never again will she have to worry about another bitch. Toya has made her point loud and clear. I spent the rest of the night cleaning up the mess as Toya slept peacefully in the guest room. This shit didn't go at all as I had planned.

CHAPTER 17

Trey

After a long night of investigating homicides, I went home and crashed on the couch. I'm not proud of my double life, but I have to look out for my sister and Sonya. My mom made a pact with me, that if I did something positive with my life, she would go to rehab. I'm stuck between good and evil. I spent all morning and part of the afternoon tossing and turning. Nightmares of Toya and Sonya both covered in blood invaded my mind. One of them was dead and the other was holding a blade, but I woke up before I could see which one was holding the blade and which one was dead.

I called Toya immediately to see if she was okay. She didn't answer the phone, so I called again. "Hello?" Toya answered.

"Hey, sis. Were you still sleep?"

"No, I'm awake. What's up, Trey?"

"I'm just checking on you. You never call me, so I have to call you," I tell her.

"You know I been busy, bro. Don't charge it to my heart. You know I love you," Toya explains.

"I guess I can give you a pass, but you need to make an effort on reaching out to me at least once a day. You got me up here stressing."

"I agree with you; I do need to call and let you know that I'm fine. My bad, bro. You forgive me?" Toya asks.

"You know I do. I love you, sis. Don't make me have to make a trip down there 'cause you won't answer the phone. Talk to you later."

"Alright, Trey. I love you too," Toya says and hangs up.

After talking to Toya I felt a little better, but I still had to check up on Sonya. I know I should have told Toya about Angelo, but I didn't want her to worry about something that I can handle. I call Sonya next and she answers on the second ring.

"What's up, Trey?" she answers.

"Just checking in with you. How is everything going?" I ask.

"Everything is on the up and up. I got the new club in control and money is still rolling in like clock work. How are you holding up on your end?" Sonya asks.

"Same here. No complaints," I reply. I had the urge to tell Sonya about my visitor from last night, but I feel it's best that I look more into it first. "I'll holla at you later. Just touching bases with you," I tell her.

"Okay, well I'm on my way to grab something to eat. Talk to you soon," Sonya says and hangs up.

It's time to get my day started, so I head to the bathroom to take a shower and brush my teeth. Afterwards, I get dressed and head out to get something to eat.

I don't have much of an appetite. I know Toya and Sonya are fine, but something about that dream seemed too real. Instead of eating a whole meal, I grab some crab-flavored UTZ chips, a soda, and a Hershey bar. On the way to Woodlawn, I eat my little lunch and mentally prepare myself for business. As I'm pulling up to the spot, I see one of my guys being pummeled by three niggas. What the fuck is going on? I grab my glock and jump out the car.

"Yo! Get the fuck off him," I shout. They act like they didn't hear me, so I shoot one into the air. All three of them begin to scatter like roaches and my guy jumps up as if nothing happened to him. "What the fuck was that about?" I ask him.

"Yo, Trey. These niggas trippin' on some shit about a nigga named Angelo. They said you better get in touch with him or else. I don't know what that's suppose to mean," he explains.

"Aight, well, go ahead and go home. I reach into my pocket and pull out my wallet. "Here's your pay for the day. Take it easy." I hand him five hundred for his troubles. "Good lookin' out yo," he says and speed walks away.

This Angelo character is pushing my buttons. I need to nip this situation in the bud, so I reach for my phone and search my wallet for his card. The phone rings and goes to voicemail,

"Yo, I don't know what kind of games you playin', but you got one more time to send your little goons to my spot and there's gonna be some serious problems for you. Nigga, you tryin' my fuckin' patience!" I hang up and head into the spot.

***

Angelo

I started my day off with a smile on my face. I finally got in touch with Trey and I have Sonya eating out of the palm of my hand. Things couldn't be working out any better. Today I'm having lunch with fine ass Sonya, stupid bitch. She has no idea who she's dealing with, but she will soon find out. I arrived an hour early to the spot she and I agreed to meet up at for lunch to keep an eye out for anything funny. I don't know if Trey told her anything yet or if he even planned on telling her at all. It'll be his mistake if he doesn't.

About an hour later, Sonya parks and gets out of her Benz. I can't lie; she is one bad ass bitch. Imma have fun with this bitch before I kill her, Trey, and Toya.

"Good afternoon love," I stand up and greet her with a kiss to the hand.

"Hey, handsome. How are you doing today?" she asks as I pull out her chair for her. "Much better now that I'm in the presence of such a beautiful woman," I reply.

She smiles and blushes up at me. As I take my seat, I notice something different about her. "Different perfume?" I ask.

"Wow, you're good. You notice everything. Like last night. You heard the music in the background and knew that I was in the tub as well. You pay close attention to detail. I like that," she compliments. Little does she know, I don't take notice of the small things to impress her.

Our lunch date went well. Sonya had the ox tail, rice, and cabbage. I ordered the jerk chicken; it was delicious and the conversation was good. Under different circumstances, I could see me being with Sonya. Unfortunately, her friend is an evil, sneaky, treacherous bitch and everyone knows that birds of a feather flock together.

"So what do you like to do for fun?" Sonya asks.

"Believe it or not, I love to read. I'm a firm believer in feeding the mind. Knowledge is power," I answer.

Sonya seemed a little impressed with my answer. "You don't strike me as the reading type. Not saying you're dumb or anything. Just caught me off guard with that answer," she replies.

"So exactly what do I strike you as?" I ask her.

"The get money type. Smooth, street smart, cunning, and of course, charming. You might be bad for my health Mr. Wettles." She laughs. I laugh with her, more like at her. She has no clue how right she really is.

As I walk Sonya to her car, I catch a few lustful looks from her and my phone rings. I send Trey to voicemail and focus on Sonya. "So uh. What about a nightcap tonight? Nothing sexual, just good conversation over a drink," I suggest.

"I wouldn't mind spending some more time with you. My place or yours?" Sonya asks.

"How about mine? I wouldn't want your man, Marques, tripping on you."

A shocked look comes over her face. "How do you know about him?"

"Ahh. See? I know much more than you think. When I'm diggin' on a female, I do my research on her to see if she's worth my time and effort," I tell her.

"Oh, really? Well, Dick Tracy, please tell me about myself."
Sonya giggles.

"You have a best friend named Toya, and you like nice
things; you're a collector of handguns. You're a go-getter and you
hate being underestimated. Am I right?" I smile.

"Damn, you're good. Let me find out you're some kind of
crazy stalker," Sonya jokes.

"Laugh now, cry later. You'll be the one stalking me. Watch
and see," I smirk.

After our little convo, Sonya gets in her car and drives off.
Our plans to meet up tonight came right on time. My plan couldn't
have worked out any better. I was one step closer to Toya, and one
step closer to revenge.

CHAPTER 18

Marques

"Daddy. Did you like school when you were little?" M.J. asks me as we walk to the bus stop.

"I loved school. Why you ask? You don't like school?"

"Well, there's this kid in my class that keeps picking on me, so I guess I don't like going to school," he replies.

"What's his name?" I ask.

"Her name is Semaj and she's always hitting on me. Can I hit her back, Daddy?"

"I think she might like you, son. Sometimes when a girl likes you, she'll pick on you. Don't hit her back; real men don't hit women," I reply.

The bus pulls up and M.J. turns to me. "Daddy, I'm a man so I won't hit her back."

"Good choice, now get on the bus. We'll talk some more later."

After watching the bus drive off, my phone rings. It's Sonya, but I don't answer. As far as I'm concerned, everything in Bmore is a closed chapter in my life. My focus is now on my family and making a decent living to provide for them. I have one last thing I need to do first. I figured I'd handle business while Bernadette is at work.

Taking a deep breath, I pull out my phone and make a call to the stash spot on Edmund Street. "Yo!" Jessup answers.

"I'm on my way to get the count. Make sure you have everything ready for me," I tell him.

"Sonya ain't called and told us nothing 'bout y'all coming through today," Jessup responds.

"Nigga, I don't have time for bullshit. Have my bags packed and ready when I get there," I order him.

"Yeah, whatever son!" He hangs up.

Before leaving the house, I write Bernadette a note.

Going out to grab some clothes and things I need here at the house. Call me if you make it home before I do. I love you. P.S. I think our son has a secret admirer at school. - Marques.

I place the note on the dining room table and head out to make one last run. All I need to get us straight is a few dollars to get us out of Maryland and buy a house. I need a fresh start and I can't do that if I'm still here. I know Bernadette would love a change of scenery. On the way to Edmund Street, I stop by Getty to get something to drink. For some odd reason I feel a little uneasy, like someone is watching my every move. Maybe I'm just being paranoid because of what I plan on doing in the next few minutes. I'm hoping that no one gives me any problems with this pick up. When I arrive at my destination, a few old friends wave at me; some just stare at me with blank looks like they know something that I don't know.

As I approach the door I take notice of Jessup watching me through the blinds. After three knocks, a females voice yells, "Who is it?"

"This is Josiah. I have some raffle tickets for sale," I reply.

The door slowly opens to the sight of a heavyset female pointing a sawed off shotgun directly in my face. "What's up, Doneisha? Everything good?" I ask her.

"Yeah, everything's straight. They got us on alert; Trey talking about keeping an eye out for trouble. Must be some shit about to go down," she says.

I shake my head at the news. "You got my luggage ready?"

"Jessup! You're needed downstairs!" Doneisha shouts upstairs.

Jessup walks down the stairs and gives me dap. "What's good, yo?"

"Just handling business as usual. Y'all got my package ready? I'm on a time limit and can't fuck around with y'all as usual," I tell him.

Jessup walks to the back of the house and returns with a black duffle bag. "I tried to check in with Sonya, but she ain't answer. Trey still hasn't returned my call yet, so you free to take it. To be honest, I don't feel comfortable giving you this 'cause Sonya ain't call and tell me nothing about a pick up today," he says with a skeptical look on his face.

"Nigga, I been doing these pick ups for years; I had ample amounts of opportunity to do dirt. Miss me with the shit," I tell him with an insulted look on my face. I grab the duffle bag out of his hand and walk out to my car. Doneisha watches me pull off; I'm definitely not feeling right.

I have four hours left to do what I have to do and get back to the house around the same time as Bernadette. My phone begins to ring as I hit Route 40. "I'm on my way there now. I got the money for you." The person on the other end hangs up on me.

Within fifteen minutes, I'm parking in front of an apartment in Edgewood. I swear to God that if this goes well, I'll be square for the rest of my life. Once again I approach the door and knock. "Hold on a second!" a guy shouts.

After three minutes of waiting on someone to come to the door, I grow irritated and knock again. This time an average-sized Puerto Rican guy opens the door. "Alberto?" I ask. "Yeah, come in. Angelo said you were gonna be coming by to drop off a package," he says in a New York accent.

"I got it right here; the agreement was fifty-fifty," I tell him as I hold up the duffle bag. "Yeah, have a seat at the table while I get my money counter." Alberto points towards the dining room table. I sit down and he walks to a room behind me to get his machine. Five minutes later I feel a sharp pain in the back of my head and everything goes black.

***

Toya

I don't know why Clyde thought I was really going to share him with another bitch, but I'm selfish when it comes to my man. He must have fell and bumped his damn head. I knew Michelle wasn't his cousin and for both of them to insult my intelligence had me peeved. I hope he learned his lesson last night when he had to clean up the mess by himself. I must say, I slept very well. By the time I woke up, Clyde was still cleaning up after our fun filled night. The bed was completely gone and so was Michelle—good riddance.

"I take it we have to go shopping for a new bed?" I asked Clyde as I walked up behind him.

He jumped in fear. "Don't sneak up on me like dat, damn!" he said in an irritated voice.

"Do I scare you honey? Aww, I sawwy." I pouted and laughed.

Clyde sucked his teeth in annoyance. "Whatever, Toya. You done pissed me off wit dat stunt you pulled last night. Why you gone do some stupid shit like dat? Why even offer to have a threesome, if you was just gone kill da bitch?" he asked.

"First off, don't get mad at me about some bullshit YOU started! I came down here to be with you and to make money. You should have left that bitch alone the moment I boarded the muthafuckin' plane! Secondly, I meant what the fuck I said last night. If you try to pull some shit like that with me again, Imma kill you, your momma, your daddy, sister, cousins, EVERY FUCKIN' BODY! You understand what the hell I'm saying? 'Cause this is the last time I'm saying this!" I shout in his face.

Clyde doesn't answer; he just shakes his head and goes back to cleaning up.

"Ignore me if you want to, but I mean what I say and I say what I mean," I say as I walk off to take a shower.

After getting cleaned and dolled up, Clyde jumped in the shower. He was finally done cleaning up the crime scene. When he finished with his shower I told him to get dressed so we could go bed shopping.

"Mane, I'm 'bout to go to sleep! I'm tired as a muthafucka," Clyde complains.

"I don't give a fuck what you are. We need a new bed and it's not gonna buy itself. Now get dressed and let's go!" I order him.

I don't care about him being tired. He didn't give a damn about my feelings when he decided to fuck with another bitch. After twenty minutes of waiting for Clyde to get ready, we were out the door and headed to MacArthur Drive for some shopping. We didn't speak the whole way there; that was fine by me. Just to piss him off more, I toyed with his feelings while shopping. The salesperson showed us a few beds and mattresses.

"I like this one. How much is it?" I ask the sales lady.

"Twenty-five hundred with the mattress and box spring included," she replied. "What do you think honey? It's real wood and it's so big. Big enough to fit three people," I say with a smile.

Clyde picks up on my sarcasm and pinches the bridge of his nose. "Look, I got a headache. Just get whatever so we can go!" he says.

I laugh and shake the sale lady's hand. "We'll take it. When can it be delivered?"

"We will be there tomorrow between one and three," she answered.

After paying the woman, Clyde and I go home. He thought he was coming home to sleep, but I had other plans. As Clyde laid in the guest room, I sat down in the living room to watch TV long enough for him to be in a deep sleep. An hour later, I tiptoed into the room and pulled down the blanket. As Clyde snored, I removed his boxers and began to suck on his dick like a lollipop. Clyde squirms a little bit and goes back to snoring, so I suck harder.

"What you doin'? I'm tired, Toya. Why you fuckin' wit' me? You know you doin' all dis to get under my skin. I ain't got time for yo shit. Guh, move!" Clyde nudges me away.

I laugh at his sensitive ass. "What kind of nigga turns down head?"

I climb off the bed and go back into the living room to watch TV, turning the volume all the way up. Clyde comes marching into the living room, beyond pissed off.

"Da fuck is yo problem? You really tryin' me and I don't know how much more I can take of yo shit! You must want me to lay hands on you!" Clyde yells and turns off the TV.

"You're not putting your hands on shit! You better remember who you're talking to! Better yet, if you ever threaten me again, it'll be your last!" I scream and turn the TV back on.

Clyde knew he was playing with fire, so he tries to make peace. "Bae, I'm sorry about Michelle, lying, hurting you, and everything else. Just please, turn down the volume so I can get some sleep, please!" Clyde begs.

"Sure, I'll turn it down. All I wanted was a damn apology in the first place. Don't let it happen again, Clyde."

"You got dat! It won't happen again, bae. Now can I go to sleep?" he asks.

"Go on and get some rest, you're gonna need it 'cause I'm horny. All that blood from last night made me horny." I laugh.

"Yo ass crazy." Clyde laughs nervously. Poor Clyde has no idea that I was actually being honest.

CHAPTER 19

Mookie

Today I decided it was a good idea to stop by Marques's house. I have to see Toya and only hell will stop me from doing so. When I get to the house, I notice that it's really quiet as if no one is home. Both cars are in the driveway, so I know they're home. I listen a little more closely and hear the TV so they must be in the living room. I knock on the door and wait for someone to answer. A few seconds later Toya, the love of my life, opens the door.

"What's good, Toya? Clyde busy?" I ask her.

"Come in, Mookie. Clyde is sleeping; he had a rough night so I don't think he'll be up anytime soon," she replies. I have a seat on the sofa and get comfortable. "What you doing? I told you that he's sleep. That's your cue to leave," Toya points to the door.

"Damn, I thought I was welcome here. I just needed to get out the house and figured I'd come here. You got a problem with me chillin' here?" I ask her.

Toya puts her hands on her hips. "As a matter of fact, I do. If Clyde didn't tell you to come over, then you need to go. There is no point in you chillin' here if he's asleep." She smirks.

"Damn, it's like dat? What if I really came here to see you? Then am I welcome to stay for a little while?" I stand up and walk towards Toya; the glint in her eye screams danger but I don't care.

"Why are you walking up on me like you know me? Listen, you're Clyde's friend, not mine. I don't know who you think you're dealing with but..." I don't let her finish her sentence; instead, I lean in and kiss her.

Toya slaps the soul out of me. "What the fuck is wrong..."

She starts to protest again, so I kiss her. This time she slaps me harder; it turns me on. Toya realizes that the pain she's inflicting on me gets me hot. I grab her hand and make her grab my dick through my sweat pants. Her eyes grow wide; obviously she is impressed with the size. A crazy look overcomes her face as she squeezes harder and harder.

"I think you tryin' to hurt me, Ms. Toya," I say with a smile. I'm starting to realize that she's just as screwed up as me and this is my signal to kiss her again. This time she pushes my face away.

"I don't kiss. Use those lips on something else besides my face," she tells me and pushes me down to my knees. I know what she wants and I'm willing to give it to her. Toya pulls down her shorts and panties, and then throws them to the side. Without hesitation, I dive in and begin to lick her pussy as she stands there. Toya places one of her legs on the coffee table so that I can get all of it.

"You been wanting this pussy, huh, bitch?" she asks me.

I begin to talk shit back, never taking my mouth off of her. This drives her crazy.

"Yeah, talk to the pussy. Tell her how much you love her," Toya moans and grabs my head.

The more she grinds into my face, the harder my dick gets. I can hardly breathe, but it doesn't stop me from bringing her to an orgasm.

"Swallow all that pussy juice, you nasty muthafucka!" she commands. She holds my head firmly and creams all over my tongue, mouth, and nose.

The taste and smell of her makes me want her even more. "You want to fuck me right here?" she asks.

I grab my rock hard dick and nod my head. "Yeah, I do. Not right now though. I want you to want it too," I tell her as I walk to the door.

"I wasn't going to fuck you; don't get cocky." She smirks at me.

At that moment, I know I got her exactly where I want her. She and I are two peas in a pod. She likes to inflict pain; it turns her on. The moment she realized that I was the same way, it intrigued her. I wink at her and walk out the door, never looking back. As I drive home, visions of what I wanted to do to her play around in my head. I'm gonna have fun with Toya, that's for sure. I might even fuck around and fall in love as well. Damn, that pussy was so sweet; the smell still lingered in my nose. I didn't bother to wipe my face off, because I have plans for all the cum that dried up on my face.

When I get home, Angela is sleeping on the couch exhausted from the dick down I gave her before I left the house. I've been fucking the shit out of her for the past two days and plan on doing it again. I kick off my shoes and remove all of my clothes, prepared to do damage.

"Wake up, bitch!" I nudge her, but she doesn't wake up. I walk to the kitchen and pour myself a glass of cold water and take a handful of ice out of the freezer to add to my glass. Instead of drinking it, I walk up to the couch and pour all of it on Angela.

"Mookie! Why you do that? You know I'm tired, bae!" she complains.

I laugh. "Bitch, I told you to get up. I don't give a damn 'bout you bein' tired. Wake up! I need my dick sucked."

Angela begins to cry, scared of what the outcome will be.

"What I tell you 'bout all that bitch ass cryin'?" I smack her across the face. Angela, quickly gets on her knees and does as she is told. Tears streak down her face and I fuck her mouth, ignoring her gagging. "You bet not throw up on my shit; bite it." I order her and pop her on the back of her head.

She bites in my dick gently at first.

"Bite harder," I command.

Angela bites down a little harder. "Good girl, now swallow daddy's dick. Get it nice and wet," I instruct her.

She deep throats my shit and the sight of her swollen lips around my shaft drives me insane. "Doggy style, on the floor now," I say to her and point to the floor.

"I'm still hurtin', Mookie! Please don't make me do this right now," Angela begs. I ignore her plea and kick her down to the floor. "Do what da fuck I said! I'm not gone ask again," I yell at her.

Angela turns over on all fours and I straddle her froggy-style with no lube. Her pussy is swollen and dry from the abuse it had to endure the past couple of days. I grab her by her hair. "You better make this pussy wet for me," I threaten.

She spits in her hand and lubricates her pussy for me. I bend down some more and tell her to lick my face and suck my lips. "It taste good, huh?" I ask her.

Angela doesn't answer me so I punch her in the back. She falls flat to the floor. "Get da hell up, Angela!" I shout at her.

Angela gets back on all fours and looks back at me with sorrow in her eyes.

"Now, I asked you a damn question. It taste good, don't it?" I ask again.

"Yes daddy, it tastes good," she replies.

"I know it do; all that sweetness came from Toya. I'll make sure to tell her that you said thank you for the treat," I tell her and smack her on the ass.

After two hours of sexual gratification, I finally cum all over Angel's back and go to the bathroom to wash up. When I get back in the living room, she's laying on the floor. The sight of her bloody knees, swollen lips, wild hair, and puffy eyes turns me on. "You ready for round two?"

***

Angela

I'm so tired of trying to be good to a nigga that treats me so bad. I can't figure out for the life of me, why I still deal with his shit. At the beginning everything was so good between us. I don't know where we went wrong. What did I do to him that would make him treat me this way? Plenty of times I thought about calling my brother Clyde and telling him what's been going on, but I don't want Mookie to get hurt. I just want him to love me the way he used to. I lie to myself over and over again, that he will change. I tell myself to just give it time and things will get better. Mookie can be so sweet to me, but then he gets his little moments where he can't help but to act out. I understand that his childhood was horrible and that's why I'm willing to stick it out.

By next week, he'll buy me some flowers and a card, maybe even a piece of jewelry and beg for my forgiveness. It's a never-ending cycle of love and hate. The question is, am I willing to go through this again? I can't blame anyone but myself for putting up with it. I know I deserve much better. Lord, what do I do? Please give me a sign, 'cause I can't take the abuse much longer. The punches are getting harder, the hate is getting stronger, and I'm scared he might kill me one day. All these thoughts are running through my head as he rapes and beats me over and over again.

Finally, later on that evening, Mookie must have had enough. He goes to the bathroom to take a shower and get dressed. "I'm going to get a drink, don't wait up," he says and he walks out the door without even glancing at me.

I'm relieved that he's gone for the night. Any other female would have cursed him out for even leaving like that, but I know that as long as he's gone, I can have some peace. As soon as I hear his car pull off, I pull myself off of the floor and go to the bathroom to tend to my wounds.

My knees are bloody from being on a hardwood floor for hours; my head is sore from all the hair pulling and punches, my lip is busted from being smacked, and there are many more things that I care less to mention. I just fucking give the fuck up! I'm so tired of his shit! Just then, my phone rings, so I walk to the bedroom to get it off the charger. It's Clyde.

"Hello?" I answer.

"Hey sis, where Mookie? Toya said he came by while I was sleep, but he ain't answering his phone," Clyde asks.

"Well, hey, to you too. Nice to finally hear from you after two whole weeks. You act like I live in another state and can't come see me," I shout at him.

"Whoa!, Hold up. Who pissed in yo Kool-Aid?" Clyde asks. "Matter fact, I'm comin' over. That way you can't say I don't ever come see you. Imma bring Toya wit' me so you can meet her," he says and hangs up.

He didn't even give me time to tell him not to come. I rush to take a shower and get dressed before he pops up. An hour later the doorbell rings and I look in the peephole to make sure it's Clyde. I open the door and there he is standing hand in hand with a beautiful redbone. I'm assuming it's Toya; the same bitch that got my man acting stupid. I can see why he's infatuated with her, but I can't see why she would even look twice at Mookie. She can have anyone she wants.

"You gone let us in or just stare all in my guh's face?" Clyde asks.

"Oh, my bad. Y'all come in and have a seat." I hold the door open for them. Toya smiles and shakes my hand. "I'm Toya. It's nice to finally meet you, Angela. I've heard so much about you," she says.

"Oh, yeah? I'm surprised because my brother acts like I don't exist, " I reply and smirk at Clyde.

Toya sits down next to Clyde and grabs his hand. Something about this girl doesn't sit right with me. I don't know what it is, but I can sense danger. I know this proper ass, stuck up bitch better not hurt my brother, that's for sure.

"So, Toya. Mookie has told me a lot about you," I say to her.

Her eyes squint at me as if warning me to keep my mouth shut. "I've had the pleasure of meeting Mookie a few times. He and Clyde are good friends. As a matter of fact, Mookie comes by a lot." She smiles.

This bitch knows what she's doing; I can see right through her. "I'll be right back. Help yourself to a drink," I tell Clyde and head to the bathroom.

I look in the mirror above the sink and take deep breaths. I was trying to hold my composure around this hoe, but it's getting harder and harder the more she talks. I grab the Listerine off of the sink, take a big swig of it, and begin to gargle. Mookie made me lick his face and suck his lips. Said it was a treat from Toya, now I know exactly what he meant. Ugh! Imma kill 'em, both of 'em, if it's the last fucking thing I do! First, I need to warn my brother before he finds out on his own. I hope Clyde kills him for me; that way all I have to do is focus on killing Toya!

CHAPTER 20

Sonya

It's been a long day and I just want to relax with Angelo. On the way home to shower and prepare for our nightcap, I check my voicemails. One of the messages catches me off guard. "WHAT?" I hurry up and dial the number back.

Jessup answers the phone on the first ring, "Hey Sonya."

"Now tell me again, what happened?" I ask.

"Your man, Marques, came by to do a withdrawal today. I was calling you to see if that's what you wanted, but you ain't answer the phone," he tells me.

"Did you give it to him?" I ask.

"Yeah, I figured it was okay 'cause he always does the pick ups. At first I thought it was a little fishy because you always call ahead of time. I called you, but didn't get an answer," he explains.

"Shit! Okay, let me call him and find out what's going on. I didn't tell him to come get shit. He hasn't been home either. Something ain't right," I tell Jessup and hang up the phone. I speed dial Marques but he doesn't answer. After three attempts, I gave up and left a voice mail,

"I don't know where you been or what you been doing. I don't care; I just want to know why you took it upon to yourself to do a withdrawal from the bank without telling me first! Then you go M.I.A. with the money? I hope for your sake, that you pop up soon with it or Toya will have your head. Call me back!"

I hang up the phone, feeling stressed beyond belief.

When I arrive home, I head straight for the bathroom and strip down. I really need this hot shower. My nerves are on edge and Marques is pinching each and every one of them. After washing up, I brush and floss my teeth then get dressed in some red leggings, a tight fitted white tee, and a pair of black and red Jordans. I put my hair in a high ponytail and place some large hoops in my ears. A little bit of natural colored shadow, some eyeliner, and lip gloss goes a long way. I take one last look in the mirror and I'm pleased with what I see, simple and sexy. I'm still stressed out, but you would never be able to tell.

Before leaving my condo, I send Trey a text message explaining what Jessup told me. I pray that Marques calls me soon. If he's up to some funny shit, there will be nothing I can do to save him. I wouldn't want to save him as a matter of fact. Toya and Trey come before any nigga, no matter the situation.

Before pulling out of my parking space, I call Angelo to get his address. He gives me an address in Upper Marlboro and I enter it into my GPS. Finally, I arrive at a beautiful neighborhood with well-manicured lawns and huge homes. The GPS sends me straight to Angelo's driveway, so I call him.

"I'm outside," I tell him when he answers.

"I'm on my way out," he tells me and hangs up. Shortly after hanging up, Angelo walks out the house and walks to my door to open it for me.

"Good evening, Queen."

"Hey, handsome. I love your home," I compliment him.

"It's a little something, something." He smiles and leads me into the house. Angelo gives me a small tour of the house; some rooms he didn't show me. One room stood out to me the most. It required a four-digit code to unlock the door. He didn't bother showing it to me. I assume it must be some kind of safe for his valuables. Anyway, Angelo and I shared a bottle of Henny between the two of us. By the time we were done, I felt nice and tipsy. Angelo and I talked all night about any and everything; he really made me feel comfortable.

Time seems to stand still when I'm with him and he always finds a way to make me blush. Angelo is everything I could ever wish for and more. "I love this song!" I tell him as I stand up to dance.

The nineties slow jam puts me in a daze as I put on a show for Angelo. He sits back and enjoys the show that I put on for him, biting his bottom lip. I straddle him and grind nice and slow, tempted to bite his lip for him. Angelo must have read my mind when he leaned forward and began to kiss me passionately. The sweetness of the Henny on his tongue brings me to a whole new level of ecstasy.

I break our kiss and tell him that I want him so bad. Angelo picks me up while I'm still straddling him and carries me up the stairs to his bedroom. I can't wait to feel him deep inside me; I've wanted him from the moment I first saw him. Angelo places me on his bed and begins to undress me slowly, kissing every inch of my body. His lips send tingles down my spine and his hands feel like silk cascading down my body. The anticipation drives me crazy, so I begin to remove his clothes. The sight of his manhood makes me anxious; he's huge!

"Are you sure that you're ready for this?" he asks. I nod my head and lay back to give him full access to my body. Angelo climbs on top of me and begins to lick and suck on my breasts as his hand massages my clit.

"Please, Angelo. Just give it to me," I beg.

He doesn't respond, instead he kisses me down to my naval. At this point I'm going crazy, grinding against his finger. All of a sudden he stops and stands up.

"Why are you teasing me?" I whine.

Angelo walks away and opens his closet. He returns with three ties in his hand. "Move up the bed," is all he says to me. I do as I'm told and he uses the ties to bind my hands to the headboard.

"What's that tie for?" I ask him. Without saying a word, Angelo takes the last tie and blindfolds me. He took away my sense of sight, strengthening my other senses. "Oh, my God!" I moan.

I can feel him French kissing my pussy; Lord have mercy. I try to reach down to play with my nipples, forgetting that my hands are tied. Feeling helpless, I lay there and enjoy the ride that he's sending me on. If his head game is this good, I wonder how good his stroke is. He has the size, but does he know how to use it?

Angelo brings me to an orgasm and climbs back on top of me. He's not doing anything, "What are you doing?" I ask.

No response. I begin to feel really nervous, but then I hear him opening what sounds like a condom wrapper. Before I can say anything else, Angelo enters me slowly. I can feel my walls stretching as he tries to fit into me bit by bit. I invite the pain and pleasure, opening my legs a little wider. After five minutes of working himself into me gently, and opening me up, he begins to speed up a bit.

I can't control myself, cumming back to back. The continuous orgasms send me into a frenzy. I want to touch him, scratch his back, and touch myself, but I can't. "Angelo, please untie me. I can't take it!" I beg but it falls on deaf ears.

He keeps dicking me down, without a single word. This is the best sex I've EVER had! Angelo was made for me; he knows my body better than I do. Finally, he speaks, "This pussy feels good, ma. Can you feel me in your stomach?" he asks.

"Yes, baby. I can feel all of you. I love this dick!" I scream.

Angelo speeds up and I begin to squirt over and over again. I think I'm in love with this nigga. "Had enough yet?" he asks. I don't answer him, causing him to go harder. The pain shoots up my back. "Had enough?" he asks again.

"Yes, baby. Please! I tap out!" I scream at the top of lungs. Angelo speeds up even faster, going harder and harder. He's killing me! I can tell he's on the verge of cumming, so I grit my teeth and take it. All of a sudden I can feel the warmth of his nut filling up the condom.

Angelo quickly climbs off of me and I can hear him walk out of the room. I wonder what he's up to now. After five minutes of laying there, I call out to him. "I'm right here," he answers.

"Oh, I didn't hear you walk back in." I laugh. Silence. "Can you untie me now?" I ask him.

"Yeah, give me a second while I run your bath," he replies.

Now, I'm really impressed with this amazing man. I can hear the tub running in his master bathroom and him returning to the bed. Angelo climbs back on top of me.

"Baby, I think I need to chill before round two. You don't know how big you are, do you?" I joke.

Suddenly, I feel a pinch on my arm and a warm sensation shooting up my veins. I begin to relax and my body loosens up unwillingly.

"What did you do?" I slur.

"That is some black tar heroin that I bought from one of your minions. I figured you should know your own product. Right?" Angelo says as he removes my blindfold. The look on his face terrifies me as everything around me begins to fade away.

***

Trey

I spent the whole day in Woodlawn handling business. Talk about being tired! Shit, I'm exhausted. Before going home to prepare for work tonight, I stop by a local spot to get a Philly cheesesteak and some fries for dinner. What I wouldn't give for a home cooked meal! Note to self; go to mom's house for dinner tomorrow. When I make it home, I dig into my meal as if it's the last thing I will ever eat. That's when I noticed that I had a few text messages and voicemails. I check all of them and call Sonya back. She doesn't answer the phone and I become nervous after ten minutes of waiting for her to return my call. She always calls me back within ten minutes; something is wrong.

An uneasy feeling comes over me, and I hope to God that these feelings are wrong. I take a quick shower and get dressed in my suit for work. It would be another long night in homicide with no sleep, and worried sick about Sonya.

When I arrive at work, I'm greeted by some fellow detectives and a pile of cases stacked up on my desk. "Detective Cummings, we got a call that we have to go check out," Detective Flemmings tells me.

I stand up and grab my jacket off the back of my chair, mentally preparing myself for whatever it was that I was about to see. When Detective Flemmings and I arrive at the scene, there are news vans and a crowd around the perimeter. This must be pretty bad, especially if it's at the Inner Harbor. This is a tourist spot and the mayor will want this solved yesterday.

We cross the caution tape and I'm greeted by the most horrendous homicide I've ever seen in my short career and I'm sure it will be the worse of all time. Sitting on a bench was the corpse of a man that's obviously been tortured, gutted, and decapitated. His head, hands, and feet are missing. Great, this is going to take a little while to solve. I walk up to one of the police officers and tell him to move the crowd back some more before they contaminate my crime scene.

"He wasn't killed here, obviously," I tell Detective Flemmings.

"Someone is trying to send a message out there, that's for sure!" he replies.

We spent hours collecting evidence and having pictures taken of the scene. What annoys me the most is that we won't be able to identify the victim. He didn't have any distinguishing marks, tattoos, nothing! We can't get fingerprints because his hands are gone. This was a professional hit by someone that definitely wanted to send out a message. I feel for whoever pissed off the murderer or murderers.

Flemmings and I head back to headquarters to put our heads together on how to solve this crazy mess.

"Not right now! I'm here on a mission! Who's on the case?" The mayor marches in the office.

We stand up and I greet the mayor. "Ma'am, I'm Detective Cummings and this is Detective Flemmings. We are on the murder case dealing with the body at the Harbor, if that's what you are referring to." I shake her hand.

"I need this solved A.S.A.P. I don't need the bad publicity and we sure as hell cannot afford to lose our tourists. I don't care what it takes! This case is your top priority. Am I understood?" she barks.

"Yes ma'am. We are on it day and night if need be," Flemmings responds.

"Good! Now, I'm going to back home to my bed. I'll leave the press conference for the two of you." She smirks and walks out just as fast as she came.

Fuck my life; when will it ever end?

CHAPTER 21

Marques

I don't know how long I was out, but when I came to, I was tied up in a chair with Alberto sitting across from me.

"He's awake now. I'll send you a message when I'm done," he says into the phone.

I wonder who he's talking to; it must be Angelo. I swear that if I get out of this alive, I will kill Alberto and Angelo. The back of my head is throbbing, and my hands and feet are tied up so tightly that my fingertips and the tips of my toes are numb.

"What is this about, man? Angelo and I had an agreement. I came through like he told me. This shit is bad business, yo!" I tell Alberto.

"You think that nigga was gonna let you ride after what the fuck you did?" he asks me.

I have to admit that I did fuck up big time. I was best friends with his brother before Toya and Sonya came into the picture. I betrayed him for the mighty dollar and now I'm paying for my sins.

"That nigga and his brother trusted you like a brother and you pissed in their faces. You a dog ass nigga. You know what happens to dogs that bite the hand that feeds them? They get put to sleep," Alberto says.

At this point I know that I'm in trouble; my death certificate is written in stone and I know that the rest of the crew is not too far behind me. God, please let this be quick and painless. Alberto rises from his seat and walks out the room. I try to loosen the rope around my wrists, but my arms won't budge. Shit, what can I do to get out of this?

My son, Bernadette—what will happen to them? I hope that they are safe and that Angelo will show some kind of mercy by leaving them alone. I don't know how long I was sitting there, but it seemed like hours. Alberto enters the room with a glazed look in his eyes; this Puerto Rican muthafucka was in there getting high.

"I'm good now, so let's get down to the nitty gritty, shall we?" he says. "You can scream all you want, but no one will hear you." He laughs.

I guess this won't be quick then and judging by the look in his eyes, I'm in a world of trouble. Alberto walks out again and returns with a steaming hot iron. My eyes grow wide with fear and I begin to recite the Lord's Prayer.

Alberto laughs. "God ain't here, nigga. You've done nothing but the devil's work and in return the devil is here to claim you."

He presses the hot iron against my face, and then my bare chest. I scream in agony as my flesh sizzles. Alberto laughs at my pain and tosses the iron to the floor.

"Weren't you praying?" he asks.

"Fuck you, nigga!" I scream.

He stops laughing and his face grows serious. Alberto hits me with a right hook and my eye immediately swells up. "This is too easy," he says and throws the pocketknife down. Alberto grabs a bat that was sitting in the corner of the room and begins to beat me, hitting every part of my body. I can hear a few of my bones breaking and a few of my teeth flew out of my mouth.

When he finally gets tired of swinging the bat, he walks out of the room. I fall asleep from all the pain. Hours later, he reenters the room higher then before with a blunt hanging out of his mouth.

"Want a hit?" he asks. Alberto takes the blunt and presses it into my hand. "See what you did? You made my shit go out!" he yells.

He then lights the blunt and again and hits it on time, blowing the smoke in my face. Again, he puts it out on my other hand. "Just fucking kill me, bitch!" I scream at him.

"As much as I would like to put you out of your misery, I just can't. Angelo wants you to suffer and suffer you will," he says.

I begin to cry with thoughts of my son and Bernadette. I promised my son that I would be there always; I wanted to go on the straight and narrow, and be a family man. Now, it's too late and I have no one to blame but myself.

Alberto sits down in the chair across from me and lights a cigarette. "Don't you have a wife and kid?" he asks.

My eyes grow wide. "Please, man, please! Don't hurt them. They have nothing to do with this!" I beg him.

"Listen, it's not up to me. Whatever happens to them is on Angelo. Personally, I'm not in the business of hurting kids. So, it's not me that you have to worry about," Alberto tells me.

I begin to pray again for my family and their safety. Alberto stands up, "I'm going to cut off your hands and feet." He walks out the room and returns with a blowtorch and a dull machete. "Sorry it couldn't be sharper. It might take a few hacks to get the job done," he jokes and laughs.

Alberto takes the red bandana from his back pocket and gags my mouth with it.I ball up my fists as he takes the first wack at my right hand and I begin to scream. He then takes the blowtorch and burns the end of my stub. The pain is excruciating. Alberto moves to my left hand and takes another wack. I'm helpless and can't move.

"Almost done. You're taking this like a champ!" he tells me and blow torches my left stub. I pass out from the pain and awakened hours later by my phone ringing.

Alberto comes into the room. "Looks like someone is calling you. Let's see who it is. Hmm, Sonya. She's fine as hell. I can't believe Angelo is about to get some of that," he jokes. W h a t did he mean by that? Was she working with Angelo or is she in danger?

"Don't worry, buddy. She's not in cahoots with Angelo, yet. He has special plans for her." Alberto smiles. I was so caught up in what he was saying, that I didn't realize the pain shooting up my legs as well as my arms. My feet were gone as well, and lying on the floor.

"Any last words? It's time to bring this to an end," he says as he removes the bandana from my mouth.

"Please, don't let them hurt my family," I beg him one last time.

"I told you, man. I have no control over that situation," Alberto says and picks the bloody machete up from the floor. I close my eyes and begin to pray again. Darkness...

***

Clyde

It felt good to see my sister yesterday, but something seemed off. I noticed that her lips were slightly swollen and the knot on her head. I wanted to confront her about her injuries, but felt that she wouldn't be comfortable talking about it in front of Toya. I also picked up on the tension between Angela and Toya. I wonder what that was all about? The ringing of my phone disturbs my thoughts.

"What it do?" I answer.

"Hey, bo. I came by looking for you yesterday, but Toya said you were sleep. What you got goin' today?" Mookie responds.

"Shit, not a damn thing. Toya and I were going through a bad patch, but it's all good now. Imma take her to the Paragon Casino tonight. Do a little gambling, maybe eat at the buffet. You and Angela wanna join us?" I ask him.

"That's what's up. We can make it a double date. I'm sure Angela would love to get out da house," he answers.

"Aight, be ready around seven," I tell him.

"We'll be ready, just make sure you don't forget to come get us." He laughs and hangs up.

I know Toya probably wouldn't approve Mookie and Angela coming with us, but I have a reason for everything I do. Seeing how my sister and Toya been acting weird towards each other and the injuries on my sister's face made me want to see how the night would turn out. I think Mookie been putting his hands on my sister. He better hope that she tells me something different or that will be his life on the line—real talk. I don't play about mines and I will choose my sister over Mookie any day.

Now, as far as my sister and Toya, that's a little tough. I can't pick sides. My sister is grown, and she got her own life. I'm living my life with the woman I love and can't just drop her cause someone doesn't like her. I just hope that everyone gets along tonight and that my intuitions are wrong. I don't want to have to kill anybody.

Toya and I spent the day shopping for a good lawyer to put on retainer. We had three appointments set up and by the time we were done meeting each one, she decided on Bridgette Green.

"I know I made a good choice. Her credentials are amazing." Toya smiles at me as I drive us home.

When we got settled in the house, Toya and I enjoyed a movie on Netflix. An hour into the movie, Toya fell asleep on my lap and began to talk in her sleep. "You made me do it. I told you NO! NO! NO!" she screamed herself awake.

"Bae, you alright?" I ask her.

"Yeah, just a bad dream. I'll be okay," she says as she stands up and heads to the bathroom.

What is going on with her? She won't tell me anything and I'm not a mind reader. Eventually it will all come out. I just hope it doesn't drive her crazy in the long run.

Later on in the evening, Toya and I got dressed for our night out at the Casino.

"You ready, bae?" I ask her.

"Yeah. How do I look?" she asks.

Toya twirls around so that I can get a good view of her outfit. "You look better den any bitch out here. Stop worrying and let's go. We still gotta pick up my sis and Mookie," I tell her.

"Hold up. You didn't tell me they were coming with us!" Toya shouts.

"I forgot to mention it, bae. I invited them to go wit' us. Just a little double date, dat's all," I explain.

Toya sucks her teeth and walks towards the door. "Next time you need to give me a heads up so that I can mentally prepare myself to deal with other people. You know I'm not a people person! Stop pushing me into situations like this," she tells me and walks out the door. I follow behind Toya and lock the door behind me. This is going to be a long night.

CHAPTER 22

Sonya

I woke up the next morning feeling groggy. What the fuck happened? I look around at my surroundings. "Where the hell am I?"

"Oh, you're awake. Good morning, sunshine," Angelo says with a smile.

"Good morning. I didn't realize that I had fell asleep. What time is it?" I ask him.

"It's eleven and I got you some breakfast," Angelo says and points towards a nightstand with a tray.

"Thanks, but I have to go. I have a lot of things to do today." I begin to get out the bed, but Angelo stops me.

"You don't remember anything from last night?" he asks.

"I honestly can't remember much. I know I must have drunk too much. I remember us making love, but everything else is a blur," I tell him.

"Damn. Well, I'm sorry to inform you that you won't be going anywhere for awhile. See, I have some major plans for you and I need you to be open to what I'm planning. Last night I gave you a good dose of heroin and tonight I will do it again. I want you to be dependent on me for everything." He smiles.

"You did what? Why the fuck would you do that?" I scream.

Angelo walks out the room without saying a word. I get out the bed; my legs feel heavy and my head is spinning. I try to open the door, but it won't budge so I begin to bang on it. "Angelo! Let me out! Open the fucking door!" I scream but he doesn't come.

I start to feel woozy, so I run to the bathroom and begin to vomit in the toilet. After emptying the contents of my stomach, I rinse my face in the sink. He must have prepared for this. There's a toothbrush and toothpaste, towels, washcloths, and soap. He planned this for a while; he set me up! Why? What the hell is this about?

I try to regain my composure and walk to the window to try to open it. It won't open and there are bars outside of it, as well as the other window. My phone! I search frantically for my phone, but it's nowhere to be found. My clothes are gone as well; all I have is the white terry cloth robe that I'm wearing. This is some shit out of the twilight zone.

I sit back down on the bed and reach for the TV remote next to my tray of food. I flick on the television and all the channels are showing the same thing; a video of Marques being tortured flashes before my eyes. I quickly turn off the TV and begin dry heaving.

***

Toya

Almost two years after I had beat up that girl for hitting on Tek, I found out that I was pregnant. Tek was excited to hear the news and Sonya couldn't wait to be an auntie. By the time I was six months into my pregnancy, Tek had shown me the ins and outs of the drug game and eventually introduced me to his connect. We even took a trip to visit his brother, Angelo, while he was locked up. Tek and I did everything together, including making money. Pregnant or not, I wouldn't turn down the opportunity to make money, especially with a little one on the way. We had everything, cars, a house in Baltimore, and a house in Harford County. I felt on top of the world and nothing could bring me down from it or at least that's what I thought.

I was at White Marsh Mall shopping for the baby when a girl approached me with a little girl. "You don't remember me, do you?" she asked.

"Am I supposed to? Who are you?" I ask.

"You're the bitch that almost made me lose my daughter over two years ago." She points in my face. It all came to me at once; she was the girl that I had beaten up.

"Yeah, bitch! You know who I am now. Imma beat ya ass and make sure you lose that bastard for sure! This is the only baby that Tek is gonna have!" she yells and points to the little girl.

Now it all makes sense. She was confronting Tek on that snowy day because Sonya and I were there and she was pregnant with his baby. That sneaky bastard; I'm going to whoop his ass!

"You lucky I got my baby with me or I'd beat you right here!" she screams and walks off.

It didn't bother me because I knew that she had no chance against me, even on my worse day.

After a day of shopping therapy, I walked to my car with a handful of bags when I heard tires screeching to a halt. By the time I turned around to see what the commotion was, it was too late. A horribly disfigured female had taken a bat to me, hitting every part of my body, focusing mainly on my stomach. I knew who she was and to be honest I can't blame her. I did fuck up her face pretty badly. A woman that was walking out of the mall called 911 when she found me unconscious in the parking lot. I suffered a concussion, fractured rib, and I had lost the baby. That day I vowed that I wouldn't rest until I killed Tek. He fucked over the wrong bitch!

That evening Tek sat at my bedside and everyday after until I was discharged. It didn't change the fact that I wanted him dead. I didn't tell him what happened or who had done it. I didn't even tell him that I knew about the little girl. It would all come to the light soon. As my wounds healed, I continued to act as if everything was fine. I made money and developed a good relationship with Tek's connect. I even accomplished turning Marques against Tek. It was only a matter of time before I would take over everything and Tek would just be a memory. I can't get my baby back and the things he did cannot be deleted like something on a computer screen. He had to pay and he was going to pay dearly.

Finally, on the day that I was supposed to give birth to our baby, Tek and I spent the day at home. I felt depressed and laid in the bed with the blinds and curtains closed, the lights out, and the

TV off. I just laid in the dark, seething from the anger of losing my baby behind Tek's bullshit.

Tek tapped on the door and walked in the room. "Baby, get up. I know today is hard for you, but laying there isn't going to help. You need to eat something."

He opens one of the blinds and hands me a plate with steak and eggs. "It looks good, but I'm not hungry right now." I try to hand him the plate back.

"Try to eat a little bit of it, ma," he begs.

"Only if you sit and keep me company," I tell him.

Tek sat down on the edge of the bed and watched me cut small bites of my steak. "I have something that I want to talk to you about," I tell him.

"Sure. What is it?" he asks.

"That day, the day I lost the baby. I know who attacked me with the bat," I tell him.

"Who was it? Tell me so I can get at 'em! You should have been told me!" He gets up and begins to pace the room.

"Sit down, baby. You're making my nerves bad with all that pacing," I order him and he sits down. I grab his hand and hold it. "It was that girl I had cut up with the box cutter and before that, the girl I had beat up approached me in the mall with your daughter," I tell him.

"My what?" He acts surprised but I can tell that he knew he was busted.

At that very moment, I grabbed my steak knife and plunged it into his back over and over again. "You son of a bitch! I hate you! I hate you! Die! Fuck you! Cheat on me? I hate you!" I screamed as I stabbed him.

Out of breath and my arm tired, I drop the knife and walk to the bathroom to wash up. I was on autopilot for the duration of the day. I finished my food as I stared and cursed out his corpse. After filling my belly with my delicious steak, I got up to pack up my things and get rid of any traces of me being there. I closed that chapter of my life when I closed the door behind me. I went to our other home in Bmore, ready to take on a male-dominated world of drugs and murder. I knew Maryland wasn't ready for a woman like me, but they had no choice but to accept it or feel my wrath.

CHAPTER 23

Mookie

Clyde and Toya picked Angela and I up from our house to go to the Paragon Casino. I really didn't want to go, but if it gives me time to be around Toya, I'll do it. Angela was silent during the ride there and Toya was as well. Clyde seemed to be deep in thought, so the music was the only thing breaking the silence. Once we got there, all of us went to the buffet to eat before it closed. As we sat down to eat, Clyde pulled out Toya's chair for her and Angela stood there looking at me as I took my seat. She thought wrong if she thought I was about to do some corny shit like pull out her chair. All four of us made small talk as we ate our meals, and Angela and Toya secretly threw jabs at each other.

"How does it taste?" Toya asks Angela.

"Excuse me?" Angela asks.

"The food; how does it taste?" Toya smiles devilishly.

"It's a little too fishy for my liking. I don't know how anyone could ever eat dis garbage," Angela replies.

"Go get you a new plate," Clyde tells Angela.

Angela gets up from the table and walks off to get something else to eat. I look across from me and catch Toya looking at me with that same devilish smile. Angela returns with her plate and has a seat.

"How about you, Mookie? How does it taste?" Toya asks me.

"I love it! It's seasoned just the way I like it. I might have to get me another plate," I tell her.

Angela reaches under the table and pinches me; she'll have to pay for that dearly when we get home. "I'm surprised that you ain't like your food. You had it before and practically licked the plate clean," I tell Angela.

Angela suddenly stands up. "I have to use the bathroom," she said and walked off.

Toya stands up and tells us that she has to use it too. I try not to stare at her ass as she walks off. I turn to look at Clyde and he's burning a hole in my head with his eyes. He must have noticed me staring.

"What I told you 'bout lookin' at her like dat, bruh?" he asks me.

"Hey, you can't blame me for looking. You know what you got," I tell him and continue to eat.

"You're here wit' my sister. Show some damn respect. Imma end up goin' to jail tonight. Keep on wit' that bullshit, real talk!" Clyde warns me, but it falls on deaf ears.

By the time Clyde and I finished eating, Toya and Angela finally came back from the bathroom laughing and talking as if they were best friends. Something seems so fake about this situation. Clyde and I hit the black jack table as Angela and Toya play the slot machines. I walked away from black jack six hundred dollars richer and Clyde lost about a hundred.

"Let's hit the poker table. That's more of my game," Clyde tells me. He wasn't lying, because he ended up winning a total of three thousand before leaving the table. Lucky muthafucka.

We looked for the girls at the many slot machines there. About thirty minutes later, we found them playing side by side. They weren't speaking; as a matter of fact you would think that they were total strangers. They were much different from earlier when they were laughing and talking while leaving the bathroom together. They staged that shit earlier; I knew it! Now I want to know what happened in that bathroom.

"Y'all ready to go already?" Angela asks me.

"Already? Bi...Girl, it's three in the morning," I catch myself before slipping up with calling her a bitch in front of Clyde.

Toya and Angela cash out with their winnings, and then all four of us walk out to the car. The ride back home was just was quiet as the ride to the casino. The only time anyone spoke was when we said our goodbyes while being dropped off at home. As soon as we step into the house, I rip off Angela's clothes and undress myself. I spent the rest of that night fucking and beating her. That shit she pulled at the casino was unacceptable; no one disrespects my baby Toya and gets away with it. No one!

***

Bernadette

I walk into the Aberdeen Police Department and approach an officer. "Sir! I'd like to file a missing person's report," I tell her.

She leads me to the correct location and introduces me to Officer Bradford. "How can I help you ma'am?" he asks me.

"Yes, sir. My fiancé hasn't been home and won't answer his phone either. I have a sick feeling that something bad has happened to him. He wouldn't just leave our son high and dry like that. He left a note telling me that he had to pick up some things but to call him when I got home. He's not answering his phone! I think something is wrong, sir!" I ramble on.

"Hold on, calm down. I need some information from you. I need to know his name, when was he last seen, how long has he been missing, and a picture of him," Officer Bradford says.

I give him all the information that I have as he types away on his computer.

"Okay, here is some paperwork for you to fill out. Have a seat over there and bring it back to me when you're done," he instructs me.

I sit down and begin to fill out the missing person's report, with my hand shaking uncontrollably. Any tattoos? No. Any scars? Upper right shoulder from a gun shot wound. Distinguishing marks? One small, light-colored birthmark on the back of his neck in the shape of an oval and one large, dark-colored birthmark that covers underneath his left arm.

I finish up the paperwork and return to Officer Bradford with the information.

"Thank you. We will call you if we find out anything," he says and walks away with the paperwork.

I grab a card off the counter so that I can call for updates. I rush to my car and drive to Swans Meadows to pick up M.J. from the babysitter.

"Thanks so much for watching him for me at such short notice," I tell Ruby.

"Don't worry about it, girl. I enjoy spending time with M.J. He's such a sweetheart," Ruby replies as she holds her hand out for payment.

I pay her what I owe then drive home, praying that Marques will be there when I pull up. As the blue water tower comes into view, my anxiety goes into high gear. "Please let him be here," I say to myself.

I take a left and slowly drive down the small hill to the stop sign. Looking to my right, I can see that his car is not parked in the front. Maybe he parked behind the house? Who am I kidding? He never parks in the back.

I parallel park in front of my house and gather my purse, M.J.'s things, and help him out of the car. "Mommy? When is Daddy coming home? He promised that he wouldn't leave," M.J. asks me.

The tears welling up in his eyes breaks my heart. "Honey, I need you to understand that your daddy loves you more than the stars in the sky. Don't ever blame yourself for him not being here. I'm sure he will pop up soon and surprise you." I smile at him.

M.J. and I walk into the house hand in hand, with hopes of seeing Marques again.

CHAPTER 24

Angelo

While eating lunch at a local diner, in walks Alberto. I stand up to shake his hand. "Have a seat," I tell him.

Alberto sits down and a waitress approaches our table. "Would you like a menu, sir?" she asks him.

"Nah, I'm straight. I'm not gonna be here long anyway," he tells her and she walks away. I take a few more bites of my food as he sits there scrolling through his phone. "Well?" I ask him.

"Oh, everything is done. I did exactly what you told me to do," he answers.

"On display?" I ask him.

Alberto nods his head. "Yeah and I threw in a little something extra for free." He smiles.   My eyebrows raise in curiosity. "Oh, yeah? Like what?" I ask him.

"Let's just say I left him wide open," he tells me.

I knew there was a reason that I had him on my team. Alberto always goes the extra mile for me. Alberto and I have been thick as thieves since we were seventeen years old. We met in high school when he moved to Harford County from New York with his family. I started selling dope at the tender age of eleven for my older brother Joey. I would deliver the product to passersby and bring him the money. Joey taught me everything I needed to know about making money the fast way. He ran Harford County with an iron fist, but I wanted more.

By the time I was sixteen, Joey was murdered in Perryman and the family business was passed down to me. I was a seasoned vet at sixteen. I knew the ins and outs of the drug game thanks to my brother. I expanded the business from Harford County to Baltimore City with my own little team of goons. There was so much money coming in that the Bloods, Crips, and Latin Kings all worked together for the old mighty dollar. I had the bloods running Edgewood, Joppatowne, Fallston, and Bel-Air. The Crips ran Havre De Grace, Baltimore County, and P.G. County. Latin Kings were my link between Maryland and New York. No one knew about my business dealings in New York except for my closest and most trusted workers, plus the LKs.

I made it a point to stay in school, no matter how much money I had. Education was always my top priority. There's nothing worse than being hood rich and dumb. I wanted to be educated and rich. I wanted to invest my money the smart way so that my money could make more money for me. When I met Alberto, I sensed that he had a few loose screws. He and I hit it off and became the best of friends. Soon, I put him on my team as my right hand man. If there was dirt to be done, Alberto took care of it like a pro. We both got caught up at the age of twenty-five and sent to prison. Luckily, like my older brother had taught me, I did the same with our baby brother. Tek took to the family business like a moth to a flame. He was born with the blood of a hustler. Unfortunately, his life was cut short because of that treacherous bitch that he fell in love with.

Now I'm back to reclaim my throne with my right hand by my side, Alberto. "Good looking out man," I tell Alberto.

He stands up to leave. "I gotta go. I got a bitch out in New Jersey that's been waiting on papi chulo to bust that pussy open." He laughs and gives me dap.

"I'll call you when I need you, so keep your phone on you at all times," I tell him.

"Hey, you know you can count on me," he tells me.

This I know for sure; that's why he's my right hand man. Alberto leaves and I finish up my meal, and then pay the bill. On the way home, I stop by a florist shop to buy a dozen white roses and a stuffed bear. When I get home, I check the surveillance from earlier. Sonya slept all day; I'm pretty sure it's because of the heroin. Before going upstairs to see her, I pour myself a stiff drink from the bar and kick off my shoes. After two drinks, I slowly head up the stairs and approach a door that requires a code to open. I enter 6157 and the door unlocks and slides open.

There she lays, sleeping off the dope I had given her earlier this morning. The room is dark except for the little bit of light peeking through the blinds. "Sonya, wake up." She doesn't move, so I open up the blinds allowing the light to hit her face. Sonya slowly raises her hand to shield her eyes from the sun. "Wake up Sonya," I tell her again.

She rises out of the bed and approaches me. "I feel sick. Please, I need some more medicine," she begs me.

"These are for you." I hand her the roses and bear. She takes one look at them and begins to beg me again. "Don't be rude. Take the gifts and say thank you," I tell her.

Sonya looks down and takes the roses and bear from my hands. "Thank you, Angelo," she says, never taking her eyes off the floor.

"That's more like it. Now, I'm not giving you anything until you wash up and do something for yourself. I'm cooking us dinner tonight and I want you to look stunning. There are clothes in the closet for you," I tell her and turn around to leave the room.

"Please, just a little bit. I don't feel well," she begs again.

"Don't beg. You'll get what you need soon," I say as the door slides closed in front of me.

***

Toya

The night out at the casino wasn't all I had hoped it would be. I accomplished a few things, but I didn't have any fun with gambling. I like to keep my money, not give it away. The buffet was an interesting situation. I had fun toying with Angela's feelings, and Mookie even joined into the fun. Clyde was clueless as to what was going on, which made it that much more fun. When Angela went to the bathroom, I followed behind her on a mission.

As she used the bathroom, I stood in front of the sink, outside of her stall.

"I know you're in here, bitch," she says and she exits the stall. Angela turns on the sink to wash her hands while I stared a hole through her. "You think I don't know about you fucking my man?" she asked me.

I laugh and shake my head. "You have no idea what you're talking about. He begged to eat my pussy and I gave him the honor of tasting it. He was nice enough to share some with you too. You should be thanking me, bitch!" I tell her.

Something in her clicked and she came at me with her claws out. I stepped to the side and she went crashing into the wall.

"You didn't think it was gonna be that easy, did you?" I laugh.

"Fuck you! When Clyde finds out 'bout dis, he gone kill you and Mookie's cheatin' ass," she screams.

That remark pissed me off, so I cocked my arm back and punched her in the stomach. Angela hunched over and began to throw up everything she had eaten. I bend down and get in her face. "Let me tell you something, bitch! If you say so much as two words to Clyde that have anything to do with me, I'm gonna kill you in the most horrible way. You think you're going to come at me with a threat? I don't take threats lightly, so let that be the LAST one," I growl. Angela stands up and begins to rinse out her mouth at the sink and I fix my hair in the mirror.

"Now look what you made me do! I broke a damn nail fucking with you! Anyway, this is what you're gonna do. You're going to walk out of this bathroom with me as if we are the best of friends. If you want to live and if you want your brother to live, you will keep your damn mouth shut. I don't want to have to kill Clyde; I love him." I smile and pat her on the back. "Besides, you're going to be my sister-in-law one day," I tell her as I give her a bear hug. "Now straighten yourself up and let's get back to our dates, shall we?"

Angela and I walked out of that restroom like we've known each other for years. I must say, she is a great actor. She really played it off like she wasn't just puking her guts out a few minutes ago. After eating, the boys played at the tables while Angela and I played the slots. I was ready to go home, but Angela acted like the slot machines were the best thing ever invented. She talked my ear off about all the times she's won something from the casino.

"I don't give a damn about you or this casino. You can stop acting now," I tell her.

She stops talking to me for the rest of the night; that was just fine with me. By the time three o' clock rolled around, it was time to go. I couldn't wait to get home to take a shower and go to sleep. The smell of cigarettes from the casino seeped into my clothes and I'm sure that my hair reeked of smoke. When we arrived at Mookie and Angela's, Clyde got out of the car and approached his sister. I knew what he was talking to her about and if she's smart, she'd keep her mouth shut. Thirty minutes later, Clyde got back into the car with an angry scowl on his face.

The short ride home was quiet. I don't know what was said, but I pray that Clyde don't come at me with any crazy shit. I just want to take a shower and sleep. When we get home, Clyde doesn't bother opening my car door for me. He slams his door and marches towards the house. I get out of the car and follow behind him.

"What the hell is wrong with you, Clyde?" I ask him.

He unlocks the door and walks into the house. "Nothing, just got a lot on my mind. I'm sorry, bae," he tells me and walks into the bathroom to turn on the shower.

I go in our room to undress and join him in the shower. Clyde and I bathe each other in silence; worry is etched on his face. I didn't know what to say to make him feel better about whatever was bothering him. I got out of the shower, dried off, applied some lotion to my body and brushed my teeth. By the time I was done, Clyde was getting out of the shower. I got into bed and grabbed a book I was reading by Shenaka Sullivan. As I got lost in the story I was reading, Clyde climbed into bed and apologized to me for being standoffish.

"You want to talk about it?" I ask him.

"I don't know what's going on wit' Angie and she won't tell me anything. I think Mookie been puttin' his hands on my sister," he tells me.

I place my book back on my nightstand and turn towards Clyde. "What makes you think that Mookie has been hitting on her?" I ask him.

"When I went by her house, I noticed that her lips were swollen and a knot on her forehead." Clyde looks at me with tears in his eyes. I knew he was pissed and ready to kill something. "I swear, Toya. If I find out dat dis nigga been puttin' hands on my sis..." A tear trickles down his face. "Imma kill dat bitch ass nigga!" Clyde grits his teeth.

"Don't stress yourself, boo. I got this; you just worry about taking care of your sister. I'll handle the rest," I smile.

CHAPTER 25

Trey

It's been six months and I still haven't heard from Sonya or Marques. A lot of my corner boys are disappearing and I still haven't solved my case of the mutilated man at the Harbor. Someone is fucking with me and I don't have the time or patience to deal with everything on my own. I've been running the strip club, stash houses, and dealing with my own personal life. I tried to keep Toya away from the drama, but things have been falling apart ever since she left. She needs to know what's going on before there is nothing to come back home to. I reach for my phone and speed dial her number.

"Hello?" she says in a groggy voice.

"Hey sis. I need you to wake up. We need to talk; it's really serious," I tell her.

"What's going on Trey?" Her voice was fully alert now.

"Have you heard from Sonya or Marques?" I ask her.

"Now that you mention it, no!" Toya says.

See? I knew it! Something is wrong if Sonya isn't calling Toya.

"Hold on. Sonya has called me a few times. She said something about a nigga that's trying to take over my shit and her handling it. I'm not worried. I know Sonya can handle herself," Toya tells me.

That still doesn't sound right, why would Sonya just disappear like that?

"Look, something is going on up here, sis. I've been running everything on my own, plus working nights at homicide. I need you back home until we can figure out what's going on," I plead with her.

"Trey, I'm almost done down here. You have to trust me; everything will be okay. Get Gutta and Corey to help you out until further notice. Sonya will pop up when the time is right. Do whatever you gotta do to keep business running," Toya instructs me.

"Toya, you don't understand! Corner boys are going missing! There's this nigga named Angelo..." I tried to explain, but she cut me off.

"Angelo? Trey! I need you to get in touch with Sincere and Beast! Have them call me!" She sounds worried.

"What's going on, sis? You're not telling me something. You need to tell me," I plead with her. "Trey, I'm coming home. Don't tell ANYONE that I'm coming! I need you to track down Sonya, 'cause if Angelo is the guy she was talking about, she's in danger! I'll call you when I touch down," Toya says and hangs up.

Okay, I wasn't prepared for what just happened. Maybe this Angelo guy is a lot more dangerous then I thought. I should have told her about him sooner, but I can't cry over spilled milk now. Only one thing to do and that's to find this nigga and kill him. Suddenly, I had an epiphany. That body at the Harbor. Could it have been Marques?

***

Angelo

Everything I had planned at this point has worked in my favor. Sonya is eating out the palm of my hand and now I can release her back into society without worrying about her straying. Before going upstairs to give her the good news, I call Alberto up on the phone. "Angelo! What's good, bro?" he answers.

"Just calling to let you know that I'm about to release Sonya and I need you to keep tabs on her. I want to know her every move. Feel me?" I tell him.

"I got you, but what about that detective nigga that you been telling me about?" Alberto asks.

"Let him breathe for now. He's my link to Toya. You've done a great job so far with disposing of their corner boys, but now things are about to get a little harder. Are you ready for the wild ride?" I ask him.

"It ain't nothing but a thing. It's time to finally take back our shit," Alberto says. He and I talk for a few more minutes before hanging up.

Sonya was surprised that I was letting her go. She had gotten so comfortable with being in my house and getting free dope, that she didn't want to leave. "What am I gonna do, Angelo? Imma get sick out there!" Sonya says with a worried look on her face.

"I got you, ma. Just do as you're told and you won't have to worry about anything. You still got your condo; I paid on that and your bills. So everything is the same, just go about your business as if nothing happened. Okay?" I kiss her on the forehead.

Sonya nods her head and gathers all her things. After packing up her car with the clothes I had bought her, Sonya left and went back to her life. Now it's time to play with my new puppet.

I know with Alberto keeping an eye on Sonya, I would be informed of her every move. The heroin dependency plays a huge part in it as well. Knowing Sonya, she will avoid buying it on the streets at any cost for fear of people finding out that she was now a fiend. Addicts don't get treated with respect but I made sure to treat her like a woman. Sonya not only loves me, but she needs me as well. That can be a deadly combination and I plan on using her to take down her best friend Toya. A few hours after Sonya left, I got a phone call from Alberto.

"What's going on?" I ask him.

"She just pulled up at her condo. I'll keep an eye on her from this point on," he informs me.

"Good. Don't let her out of your sight," I tell him and hang up. Let the games begin.

CHAPTER 26

Toya

"Clyde, I have to go handle something back home!" I tell him while packing up my bags in a rush.

"Hold on, bae. What's wrong?" he asks me.

"Just some crazy shit is happening, and I have to go fix it before it's too late," I tell him.

Clyde rushes to his closet and begins to remove clothes.

"What are you doing?" I ask him. "I'm coming wit' you!" he tells me.

I stop packing and approach Clyde. "Baby, I need you to stay here. We accomplished so much down here and it'll all be for nothing if no one is here to run things while I'm gone." I hug him.

"Damn, bae. I really don't feel right lettin' you go back to handle it by yoself," he whines.

"I'll be fine, trust me. I have an army back home. I need you to be my eyes and ears here. Understand?" Clyde nods his head in agreement. "Good. I'll keep you posted and you keep me posted as well."

I zip up my luggage and he carries it to my car. We share a passionate kiss and a long embrace before I head to the Alexandria airport. I slept on the flight back home; nightmares of what had transpired over the past six months come tumbling at me.

"So what can you do for me? That's what I wanna know," Rob Rob asks me.

"Look, you need me, more than I need you. Trust and believe that," I tell him.

We sat in his car negotiating a business deal that I had no plans on going through with. "That's not what I mean and you know dat. Clyde my nigga and all dat, but I want some of dat pussy. You know a nigga like me can have any guh he wants. Shit, I got three girlfriends at home. I want you doe," he tells me.

"Is that right? Well, let's go somewhere a little more private then." I wink at him.

Rob Rob takes me to a crummy hotel, which makes me want to go through with my plans even more. How dare he bring me to a roach motel? The disrespect is endless with this guy. Rob Rob parked in front of the room and we got out the car. We entered room twelve; Rob Rob wasted no time unbuckling his pants.

"Straight to the nitty gritty huh?" I ask him.

He lays down on the bed and waits for me to join him. *Okay, if that's the way he wants it*, I think to myself. I reach into my purse and pull out a butcher knife. Rob Rob is so into stroking his fat little dick that he doesn't notice what I'm getting ready to do. With my hand behind my back, I climb on top of him.

"Why you still got yo clothes on?" he asks me.

Without warning, I raise my hand up over my head and bring it down with all of my strength, striking him in the face. After a few strikes to his face, I know that the job is done. I spend an hour cleaning up and walk to the nearest store to call Clyde.

"It's done, baby. Come get me at Popeyes," I tell him.

Clyde gets to me within five minutes and takes me to my car. "I told you that he was no good. He really took the bait, boo," I tell him.

Clyde shook his head. "I didn't think dat nigga was gonna try to fuck my guh. I don't feel bad 'bout what happened den. Fuck dat nigga!" Clyde yells.

Now that Rob Rob was out of the picture, it would be much easier to take over the game. That night Clyde and I made love until the next morning. He and I planned for him to tell Mookie that he was going out of town to handle something. I knew that Mookie would fall for the okie-doke. That morning Clyde left the house for the day and just as I had thought Mookie pops up that afternoon.

"Hey, Toya. Clyde here? I gotta talk to him 'bout some shit." I know that Clyde told him that he wasn't going to be home. "No, he's not here. He went out of town today," I tell him. "Oh, yeah? Well, can I come in anyway?" he asks.

"Sure, come on in. I was bored anyway," I tell him.

Mookie takes a seat on the sofa and turns on the TV. I sit next to him and he immediately begins to touch me. "Whoa. Hold on, cowboy. It's not that kind of party," I tell him and stand up.

"Damn, why you actin' like dat? Don't you wanna finish what we started?" he asks. I walk into the bathroom and he follows. "How 'bout you go pour us a drink at the bar? Some Patron, please," I tell him.

Mookie walks off to do as I asked. I turn on the shower and begin to undress. When Mookie returns to the bathroom with our drinks, his mouth opens wide. "Are you going to stare at me or join me?" I ask him.

Mookie gulps down his drink and begins to undress. After five minutes of washing me from head to toe, Mookie stops scrubbing my back. "Da room is spinnin'. I need to sit down," he complains.

"Aww. Poor thing. That must be all the Xanax I had crushed up and put in the patron bottle." I turn and smile at him.

"You bitch, " he slurs and passes out, crashing to the floor of the shower. Mookie's head begins to pour out blood from hitting his head. He's out like a light and I have plenty of time to do what needs to be done.

I get out of the shower and put my clothes back on as quickly as I can. As Mookie laid, passed out, I ran to the kitchen to grab some duffle bags, bleach, a butcher knife, and an electric saw from the storage room. The rest of the day was spent cutting him to pieces, bagging him up, and loading the truck of my car. By the time Clyde made it home, Mookie was in my trunk ready to be dumped.

"I need you to take my car and dump Mookie somewhere where he won't be found," I tell him.

Clyde doesn't ask any questions; he gets into my car and does as he is told as I clean up our bathroom. By the time I finished up everything, I was beyond tired. The turbulence from the flight back to Bmore woke me out of my nightmare. I look at my watch and realize that I still had another two hours before landing.

I tried to stay awake for the rest of the flight, but my eyes betrayed me. I fell back asleep and the nightmares continued. Clyde comes to me with some information about another local dope boy with some weight.

"His name is Big G," he tells me.

"Okay, introduce me to him and I'll handle it from there." I smile.

Clyde shakes his head. "You ain't no joke. Remind me to stay on yo good side." He laughs.

Swirls and swirls of my victims' faces come at me, then I end up in a house. Across from me sits a heavyset male stroking his dick as he watches me play with myself. "You like dat big daddy?" I ask him.

"Hell yeah, I like dat shit guh!" he tells me and begins to cough violently, and then passes gas. This nigga is disgusting and he doesn't even notice how dry I am as I play with myself. I'm not turned on in the least bit, but I'll get my rocks off when I see the light fading from his eyes.

Big G grunts and snorts as he begins to cum all over his hand. "I'm going to use your bathroom to wash up," I tell him.

I grab my purse and head to the bathroom with thoughts of cold-blooded murder on my mind. As I look through my purse, I had the hard choice of deciding if I wanted to try out the new silencer on my gun or if I wanted to break in the new twelve-inch hunting knife that Clyde had bought for me. As I walked back into the living room, Big G was watching the evening news. His back was turned towards me, so I crept up on him with my hands raised above my head, gripping the knife.

"I can see yo reflection in da TV, bitch," he tells me.

"Well, say your prayers, you fat, greasy fuck!" I scream. I blacked out and when I snapped out of my trance, the person that was once Big G was no more. "That'll be a closed casket, for sure," I say to myself, wiping the blade on his pants and putting it back in my purse.

All of a sudden, someone knocks on the door. I know that I'm caught red-handed when the door opens and there stands a tall, skinny nigga in shock.

"Da fuck?" he says and begins to reach for his waist.

My body goes into autopilot, snatching the gun out my purse and hitting the man with three slugs. Two to the chest and one to the dome. The sound of his body dropping to the floor lets me know that my job is done and that I need to hurry up and get out of there before someone else comes by.

Clyde laughed at my story that night. "Bae, you just killed two birds wit' one stone. Da tall skinny nigga that you shot was another dope boy named Orlando."

"Good. One less person to kill." I smile. Four down, two more to go. The pilot announcing our arrival to BWI airport awakened me; it was music to my ears. Home sweet home. Now it's time do some damage control.

CHAPTER 27

Bernadette

"Hello? Officer Bradford?" I speak into the phone.

"Yes, this is he. How can I help you?" he asks.

"It's been months since my fiancé disappeared and every time I call, I am given the run around. I need more answers. Is the case even being worked on?" I ask.

"I told you that we would contact you if there were any changes," he tells me.

I hang up the phone in frustration. I've called these people so damn much that they knew who I was just by my voice. I'd do a better job at finding out what happened to Marques. The whole day at work was a blur to me. Hell, the past few months have been a blur. My main focus was on taking care of M.J. and keeping it together for his sake. After this whole ordeal with Marques is over, I'm packing up and moving to Georgia. There is nothing left for me here and the family that I do have here isn't worth a shit.

Marques may not have been around much when M.J. was growing up, but he always made sure that we were taken care of financially. Now that he was gone, the bills have piled up, and it was getting harder for me to maintain everything on my own. When I found out about a new opening in Georgia that paid more, I jumped at the opportunity and received a call within a week. M.J. was excited by the news, but worried that if we left, his daddy wouldn't be able to find us. It breaks my heart that my son has to go through this. At least once a day he tells me that his daddy made a promise to him. I know deep down inside that Marques would never break a promise to our son.

After a long day of work I went to Swans Meadows to get M.J. from Ms. Ruby's house. "Mommy! I missed you!"

M.J. runs out the house and jumps into my arms. Ms. Ruby walks out behind him with his jacket and book bag. "He had an episode today. He really misses his daddy," she reports.

"I know, I know. What can I do though? I call the police station at least two times a day. That's all I can do," I tell her.

The tears in my eyes threaten to fall out, but I hold them in for fear of M.J. seeing me cry. "That's all you can do. Go to Georgia and make a better life for you and M.J. Maybe a change is what you guys really need," she says.

I know that what Ruby is saying is true; I just needed someone else to tell me what I already knew. When M.J. and I arrived home, he asked me a question before getting out of the car, "Mommy, is Daddy dead?"

"Why are you asking me that?" I ask him.

"'Cause the other kids at school keeps making fun of me. They said my daddy is dead and won't come back home." He begins to cry.

"M.J., you wipe those tears from your face, right now! Don't you ever let ANYONE pick on you. You hear me?" I shout at him.

He nods his head and wipes his tears with the back of his hand. We finally make it into our townhouse and when I flick on the lights, nothing happens. Shit! If it isn't one thing, it's another. Lord, why me? BGE gave me an extension to pay my bill because I didn't have the money to pay them, but they obviously turned everything off anyway. What can I do? Who can I call for help? I guess it's time to swallow my pride and call the only family I have left. I dial my brother's number and he answers on the first ring.

"Well, look who decided to call. How are you doing, Ms. High and Mighty? What gives me the honor of receiving a call from Ms. Holier Than Thou?" He laughs into the phone.

"Angelo, I don't have time for your shit! I need your help."

***

Sonya

It felt good to be home, but I missed Angelo. I know it seems crazy, because of what he did to me. Despite that, he treated me like a queen and made love to me like no one ever has. Now that I'm back home, I don't know what to do with myself. Angelo told me to go back to my daily routine. The first thing that came to mind was to call Trey. I had to tell him about Marques.

"Sonya?" he answered.

"Yeah it's me." I laugh nervously.

"Where the hell have you been? Do you have any idea of what's been going on?" he asked.

"Trey, stop tripping. I'm grown, so if I decide to take some time out for myself, I should be able to do so. You're not my daddy!" I yelled into the phone.

"Hold on! Don't get mad at me! You know just as well as I do, that there is a business to be run. My sister left you in charge for a reason. She trusts you and you're suppose to be her best friend!" Trey tells me.

I began to feel guilty for yelling at Trey. Deep down I knew that he was speaking the truth. "I'm sorry, Trey. I just got burnt out. I needed to regroup. I'm back now and I'm refreshed. It won't happen again. I promise," I told him.

"Well, you're a little too late now. Toya is on her way back home to handle things. Do you know a guy named Angelo?" Trey asked me and I instantly began to shake.

I wasn't ready for that conversation; I needed some medicine to cope with what Trey was throwing at me.

"Angelo? The name sounds familiar, but I don't think I do," I lied.

Trey didn't say anything as if he was deep in thought or he didn't believe me. Think, think, think! I needed to change the subject.

"I was calling to tell you about something I heard through the grapevine. Rumor has it, that Marques was tortured and killed some months back. I've tried calling him a few times, but he would never answer," I told Trey.

"I know, 'cause I'm the one working the case at homicide. I had a feeling it was him; I just didn't want to jump the gun," Trey said. "So did you hear anything about who may have done it? I'm thinking it was this Angelo cat," he inquired.

Damn! I don't want to tell him that it was Angelo that had put a hit out on Marques. "No, I didn't hear anything about who did it," I lied again.

"Aight, well I need you to meet me at the Park Heights spot in an hour. Make sure you're there Sonya!" Trey ordered and hung up on me.

The affects of withdrawal gave me chills and the pain was starting to become unbearable. I dialed Angelo's number. "Please, please, please pick up!" I beg.

"What's up?" Angelo's voice sounded like music to my ears.

"Baby, I need my medicine! I can't function and I have to meet up with someone in an hour!" I begged.

"Meet up with who and where?" he asked.

"A close friend named Trey. He wants me to meet him in Park Heights and I can't be going over there like this!" I told him.

"I'm a little busy right now, baby. You're gonna have to wait until later on tonight. Handle your business with your friend and by the time you're done, I'll be headed to your place," Angelo said.

"But..." I started to beg again, but the line went dead. Fuck! How can I go to a dope house with heroin in it without getting dope sick? This is going to be really difficult and I just pray that I'm strong enough to resist stealing.

An hour later I sat in front of the dope house, scared to get out of the car. I practically jump out of my seat when I hear someone tapping on my window. It was just Trey.

"You gonna get out of the car? We gotta handle some shit and I don't have all day to fuck around," he said.

I get out of my car slowly, trying to prolong the inevitable. My feet dragged as we headed into the house and were approached by a familiar face. Lord, I'm not ready for this! My cold chills became worse and I felt sick to my stomach. At that very moment I began to vomit uncontrollably. I ran back outside for some fresh air.

"Not happy to see me?" Toya walked up behind me.

CHAPTER 28

Toya

Despite the nightmares and bad feeling that coming back was a big mistake, I called Trey and had him pick me up from BWI airport, so that we could get straight to business. He put Sonya on speakerphone as we were riding down I-95. Something about their conversation didn't sit right with me. Sonya seemed distant, like she was hiding something. I just can't seem to shake this nagging feeling that she was up to no good. I hope for her sake, that I'm just being paranoid. Most likely, these feelings are one hundred percent correct. I've always gone with my intuition and they have never failed me. When Trey hung up with Sonya, he gave me a worried look. "You thinking what I'm thinking?" he asked me.

I nodded my head, popped my Lil Boosie CD into the radio, and stared out of the window for the rest of the ride, deep in thought.

We arrived at the Park Heights trap house ten minutes before Sonya. I noticed she parked her car, but she didn't get out. I observed her for a few minutes and came to the conclusion that she didn't want to be here.

"Trey, go get Sonya," I tell him.

Trey walks out of the house and taps on her window. I saw her jump in fear; that's not the Sonya that I know. What happened to her? I continued to watch her every move. The way her hands shook, the way she was dressed in sweat pants and a wrinkled shirt, her hair was in bad need of a perm, and she looked pale. Everything I was seeing were the signs of a fiend. I pray to God that my best friend hasn't been getting high off of our product.

Trey and Sonya walk in and the moment she saw my face, she ran outside and became ill. "Not happy to see me?" I asked her.

Sonya wouldn't turn around to face me.

"Well, damn! Can I get a little bit of respect? Can you at least look at me? I thought you would be happy to see me," I said.

Sonya hunches over and grabs her stomach.

"What's going on with you, Sonya?" I asked her. "I'm alright. I...I...got a little stomach virus that's all," she lied.

I knew she wasn't being honest and it pissed me off that not only was she being devious, but she was lying to my damn face. "Come in the house, Sonya. We got a lot of things to discuss." I grab her hand and lead her into the house.

Sonya resisted at first, but she must have thought about what she was doing and quickly straightened up. As we passed Trey on the way to the sofa, he shook his head in disappointment and followed close behind us.

The three of us sat in silence for a few minutes before I began to speak. Sonya didn't take her eyes off of the floor, occasionally scratching her arm. I don't think she realized what she was doing.

"Alright, guys. I came home because it was brought to my attention that Angelo is out of prison and as sure as I am that the sky is blue, I know that he isn't here to make friends. I'm pretty sure that he's pissed about what happened between his brother and I, but I wouldn't take back what I did if my life depended on it. If Angelo is here for a war, he found the right one to do battle with."

I noticed Sonya becoming more nervous at the mention of Angelo's name.

"Sonya, where have you been? You told me that you were following a lead. So what is it?" I asked her.

Sonya scratches her arm and looks at me. "I heard that Marques was tortured and murdered awhile back and dumped at the Inner Harbor," she said.

"I know. I heard your conversation with Trey on the way from the airport. My question is, why are you just now telling us this?" I asked.

Sonya shakes her head. "I don't know. I guess I wanted to gather some more info before coming to you guys about it," she lied.

I nod my head and look at Trey. "Give us a moment. Go upstairs and make sure everything is running smoothly. We'll meet you up there," I tell him.

Trey gets up from the sofa and walks off.

"Sonya." I grab a hold of her hands and look into her eyes. "You know I love you, right?" I ask her.

Sonya nods her head and her eyes well up with tears. "You need to tell me everything you know. I promise that no harm will come to you. We've been through too much and I won't turn my back on you. You're my sister. Just please, tell me everything you know and don't leave anything out," I said.

Sonya takes a deep breath and begins to cry uncontrollably. I hold her, allowing her to let out all of her troubles. "Toya, I didn't know who he was. We met at a diner and...and...I thought he was the perfect gentleman. He treated me like a queen; he said all of the right things," she said. I didn't interrupt her, I just held her as she poured out her heart. "It was Angelo, but I didn't know who he was. You know I would have killed him on the spot if I had known who he was and what he was all about. You believe me, don't you?" she asked.

I nod my head and she continues to tell me about their date, the video of Marques's murder, and her being trapped in Angelo's house and given heroin. By the time she was done, I was furious. I didn't let her know how angry I was, because I didn't what her to think that I blamed her.

"You're going to rehab, Sonya. Not tomorrow, but right now! We can get through this together. Don't worry about what's going on out here; you just focus on getting better. I'll handle all of your bills for you while you're gone. Just let me head upstairs to tell Trey what's going on and I'll be right back. Don't move from this couch," I told her.

I head upstairs and I'm greeted by Corey. "It's good to see you boss lady," he said in his deep baritone voice. I pat him on the shoulder and let him know that it felt good to be home.

"Where's Trey?" I asked. "In the other room, talking to Dro," he told me.

I knock on the door and Dro peeps out, and then quickly opens the door for me. "Trey, come out here. I have to talk to you," I said.

Trey comes out into the hallway and I tell him Sonya's story. "Damn, I feel bad! I should have looked for her. Fuck!" Trey shouts.

"You can't blame yourself, little bro. It's not your fault; just keep an eye on things while I take her to get some help. I'll call you when I'm done," I tell him and kiss him on the cheek.

I rode with Sonya to her condo, but on the way there, I noticed a car following us. I made a mental note to myself about the color and type of car that seemed to follow our every move. It was a red BMW with dark tinted windows, so I couldn't see who was behind the wheel. As Sonya parks the car, I see the BMW parking as well. On the way in, I look at the license plate of the red BMW. New York? It can't be one of my connects and I know for a fact that Sincere and Beast would never ride in a red BMW; it was too noticeable. They like to be incognito when they come in town. As soon as we make it into Sonya's condo safely, I call up Trey.

"You okay?" he asks nervously.

"Yeah, we're fine. Just came to pack her a bag to take to the rehab center. Do me a favor, and get one of your detective friends to run a plate for me," I said.

"Sure, what's the number?" Trey asked. "It's a red BMW, New York plate number BERRY 1. It's been following us. I need to know who's behind the wheel of that car before we walk out of this condo," I told him.

"Give me a few minutes and I'll have that info for you," he said and hung up.

Within ten minutes Trey called me back with the information I needed. "I should have known that Angelo would send Alberto to do his dirty work. Shit! Okay, I got this handled," I said and hung up before Trey could protest.

I walked into Sonya's closet and opened up her secret gun collection. I took one of her desert eagles and a Beretta, tucking them behind my pants. When I turned around, Sonya stood there looking at me.

"What? You know I couldn't bring a gun on the plane," I said to her.

"You know I have no problem with you using my guns. You're the only one that knows where my stash is for a reason. Just make sure you put them back when you're done with them," she said.

I nod my head and grab a few boxes of ammo to put in my purse. "When we walk out of here, I need you to walk straight to the car. Don't look back, just get in the car and start the engine," I instructed as I put on one of her hoodies.

Sonya nods her head and hands me a key to her place. We walk out and Sonya locks the door behind us. My mind goes into beast mode and I get tunnel vision; I was ready for whatever.

CHAPTER 29

Alberto

Sonya finally made it home so I called Angelo to let him know that she had arrived. He told me not to lose sight of her and to report back to him. I made sure that I followed her at least two cars back as she drove to Park Heights. So, this must be one of the trap houses. I might have to round up some goons to rob this place. What they gonna do? Call the police and tell them that someone robbed them for their drugs and money? Anyway, Sonya sat in her car for a little while before a nigga came and got her. When she went into the house with him, I called Angelo to let him know where we were. That's when I noticed her run back out of the house with a bitch trailing behind her.

I laugh at Sonya's fiending ass; this shit is hilarious. I try to make out who the other girl is, but they aren't close enough to tell. I speed dial Angelo to let him know what's going on. "What's good?" he asked.

"I followed her to Heights; looks like a trap house. I think that nigga Trey is here. I'm not one hundred percent positive that it's him though," I told him.

"Yeah, it's him. Stay there until she comes out so you can find out where she goes next," Angelo instructs me.

We hang up and I continue to sit and wait for Sonya to emerge from the house. When she finally came out of the house and to her car, the same bitch from before follows behind her, but Trey is nowhere in sight. Oh shit! That's Toya's fine ass. Angelo is going to be pleased when he finds out that his plan worked. I wait a few seconds before following them, making sure that Toya doesn't spot me. We ended up back at Sonya's condo, but for what? As she parks, I park five spaces away and then my phone begins to ring.

"What's good, ma?" I answer.

"Hey papi, when am I gonna see you again? I'm missing you!" Rosetta coos into the phone.

"I'm handling some business right now. I gotta call you back," I tell her. I don't know what she said back to me because I was too focused on watching Toya in my rearview.

"Did you hear anything I just said?" Rosetta asks.

"Naw, my bad. I told you that I'm handling business," I tell her.

"Okay then just call me when you have time," she tells me and hangs up.

Once again, I call Angelo to give him the good news. "Damn, you don't have to call me about every little thing. What is it now?" He sounds annoyed.

"We're back at her place again and you'll never guess who she's with," I tell him.

"Oh, yeah? Who's she with? Wait, hold that thought, I gotta answer this other line," he says and puts me on hold.

I almost hung up on him because he had me on hold for so long. He finally came back on the phone when I spotted Sonya walking to her car, but she was alone. "Who was she with?" Angelo asks.

"Hold on, bro. Where is she?" I ask out loud. I look through my rearview when all of a sudden I saw a shadow speed past the front of my car.

"Who the fuck is that?" I ask out loud.

I can hear Angelo on the other end of the phone asking me who. "Something fishy is going on. I think she's playing games with me," I tell him.

"Who the fuck are you talking about? Sonya?" Angelo shouts into the phone.

"No, not Sonya. It's..."

***

Angelo

Right when I thought Alberto was about to tell me who he was talking about, two shots rang out. "Hello? Berry! Bro, what's going on?" I ask, but he doesn't answer back.

I try to listen to what's going on in the background. "You're next," someone says into the phone and it goes dead.

"Fuck!" I shout and throw my phone in frustration. Not my nigga Berry! Who the hell was he talking about? I throw on some shoes, grab my car keys, and run out to my car. I have to get to Sonya's condo so I can find out if Berry is hurt or dead. I sped the whole way there, not worried about getting pulled over.

By the time I make it there, the place is swarming with 5-0, the ambulance, and fire department. I can't see the crime scene so I park and get out of my car. A nosey crowd formed around the caution tape as detectives collected evidence. I pushed through to the front and that's when I saw my longtime friend laid outside of his car, covered with a sheet.

Alberto was the closest thing I had to family besides my sister and the little bastard she had with bitch ass Marques. Berry was loyal to the bitter end and I swear on my life, that his death will not go in vain. There was nothing else I could do, but go home. I don't know where Sonya is, but she will pop up when that monkey on her back gets too heavy. Now who can I get to replace Albert? When I got home, I brainstormed on who liked to get their hands dirty and is very loyal. One person came to mind, so I called him.

"Who this?" he asked.

"This is Angelo. How you been old friend?"

"What's good Angelo? Shit, out here gettin' this money. When did you touch down?" he asks. "Been home for a little minute now," I tell him.

"That's what's up. Welcome home. So what do you want? I know you ain't call me just to shoot the shit." He gets straight to the point.

"I got some serious money to be made, if you're willing to partner up with me. First, I need your help with exterminating Toya and her little dick suckers," I tell him.

"You must think I'm stupid. I know about you and Toya going to war and to be honest, I don't switch sides. Plus you're the reason that I'm short a handful of corner boys. I'm here to make money and I can't make money or spend it if I'm dead. I value my life and fucking with you will solidify my death. I'm staying on Toya's good side, bro. You're on your own. I don't know how you got my number, but you need to lose it," he says and hangs up.

I knew that Gutta was as loyal as they came, so it didn't surprise me that he wouldn't take my offer. Finding a replacement for Berry was going to be much harder than I thought. I spent the rest of the night at home trying to come up with a plan. I guess I need to bite the bullet and go home. All of my loyal goons are there, but so are Toya's. The next morning, I woke up and packed an overnight back to go to Harford County. Sonya never showed up or called for her fix. So I guess it's safe to say that she is either dead or hiding from me.

It doesn't take me long to get to my destination. I never thought I'd be parked in front of her house, but she was the only family that I had left. Yeah, I could stay in a hotel but why spend money when I don't have to? I ring the doorbell and a little boy that looks just like Marques opens the door. "Where's your mom?" I ask him.

"Mom! There's some guy here to see you!" he shouts. Bernadette comes to the door and rolls her eyes at me. "Well, look what the cat drug in. What do you want, Angelo?" she asks.

"Oh! So I can send you money to get your utilities back on, but I'm not welcome here?" I ask her.

"I see that you have a duffle bag with you. I don't want any drugs in my house, Angelo!" she tells me.

I shake my head and place my bag on the ground to open it for her. She looks inside. "See? It's clothes! Now, can I come in?" I ask her.

Bernadette opens the door for me to enter. She looks as if she hasn't slept in awhile.

"You look like crap. What's going on?" I ask her.

"It's Marques. He's missing and no one is taking it seriously. I feel like no one is even looking for him," she tells me.

I begin to feel bad for her. After all, she is still my sister.

"I'm sure he'll pop up soon," I tell her. "Well, make yourself at home. I'm about to cook dinner and M.J. is in his room playing a game. Just don't bring any trouble to my doorstep Angelo!" she tells me and walks back downstairs.

I don't know why she was tripping on me. She has no idea how close she and her kid came to dying behind Marques's shit. If it weren't for me, both of them would be dead.

CHAPTER 30

Trey

I didn't feel comfortable with letting my sister and Sonya go back to the condo by themselves, knowing Angelo was out there. After they left the trap, I waited ten minutes before heading to Sonya's. Luckily I did go, because the moment I pulled up, I noticed someone in a hoodie sneaking up on a red car. All of a sudden two shots went off. The hooded assailant said something into a phone and threw it. That's when I realized that it was Toya. I rode up to her, but she didn't seem to notice me there, like she was in a trance.

"Toya!" I shouted.

She blinked and then turned and looked at me, smiling. I got out of the car to grab her. I knew that the police would soon be on their way and we had to get out of there.Before I could get to her, she turned back around and began to empty the clip into her prey.

"Let's go, right now!" I shouted as I dragged her to my car. Another car comes to a screeching haul behind mine; it's Sonya.

Toya pushes me off of her. "I can handle it! I told you to stay at the house!" she screams and gets into Sonya's car.

They speed off and I jump in my car, heading back to Park Heights. I hope to God that there weren't any cameras around to record what had just occurred. On the way back to the trap, I changed my mind and took a detour to my mom's house. I was in much need of some TLC and a home cooked meal. I just needed a break from all of the drama.

"Come in, son! How have you been, baby?" my mom asked as she opened the door. I gave her a hug and a kiss on the cheek.

"I'm doing fine, Ma. Taking it one day at a time," I told her.

"Looks like you're losing weight. Are you eating?" she asked.

"That's why I'm here, Ma. I need some of your good old fashioned southern cooking." I smile and rub my belly.

"Well, you came to the right place, 'cause I got some turnip greens, black eyed peas, beef tips, rice and gravy, corn bread, and some homemade banana pudding for dessert," she said as she ushered me into the kitchen.

My mom always cooked more than she needed so that she would have leftovers for the next few days and not have to cook. It just so happens that I caught her on a day that she was cooking. The aroma of all the food made my stomach growl and cramp up from hunger.

As I sat at the table and ate the plate that my mom had made for me, I noticed a bruise on her arm. "What happened to your arm, Ma?" I asked.

"Oh, this? You know how clumsy I can be. I fell two days ago. It's not a big deal, my baby. I think I may need some glasses. Sometimes my vision gets a little blurry and I get these bad headaches," she said and rubbed her temples.

"Yeah, you need to go to the doctor and find out what's going on," I said with concern. "This food is too good to be keeping to yourself, Ma. Have you thought about what we talked about last time?" I asked.

"Trey, I would love to start my own soul food place, but I have no idea on how to run a business. Besides, who would help me run it?" she asked.

"Ma, I told you that I would give you the funds that you need and I'm sure that Toya will help as well. I'll put an ad in the paper for people to come put in applications and hire you a lawyer too. I'm telling you that you will make a killing out here. Plus you'll be helping the community by opening up new jobs." I smiled.

"Okay, I'll make a deal with you. If you can promise me that you'll continue to do right and find you a good woman to settle down with so that you can make me some grandbabies, then and only then will I go into business with you," Mom said with her fingers crossed.

"You got a deal, Ma. Well, I gotta go home to get ready for work. The food was delicious, thank you." I gave my mom a hug and we walked to the door together, arm in arm.

You know you can come by whenever you want to. My home is your home," Mom said and kissed me on my cheek. We said our good byes and then I was on my way home to get ready for another long night in homicide. Only this time, I had all the information that I needed to solve the case. Turns out that the rabbit hole went much deeper than I had thought.

***

Sonya

"Who the fuck did you just kill?" I asked Toya.

"Slow the car down before the police pull you over for speeding. That was a guy named Alberto. Does it ring a bell?" she asked me.

I let the name roll around in my mind until I finally realized that I heard Angelo speaking to someone on the phone by the name of Alberto. "I've heard Angelo talking to an Alberto before," I told her.

Toya nodded. "That was him. Alberto a.k.a. Berry was Angelo's little errand boy. If Angelo wanted something done or someone hurt, Berry was the one he called," Toya said as she took off the hoodie.

"You don't think that he's the one that killed Marques, do you?" I asked.

"Most likely he's the one that did it. I'm pretty sure that you would have been next after Angelo was done using you," Toya replied.

Toya stared out of the window the rest of the way to the rehab center. It always worried me when she would just stare. That usually means that she is thinking of the many ways that she would like to kill someone. I left her alone to her thoughts and drove.

Once we arrived at the rehabilitation center, the staff greeted us. As Toya and I filled out the proper paperwork, they checked my belongings to make sure that I was not bringing in any contraband.

"Looks like you're ready to begin your journey," the receptionist said to me as I handed her my paperwork.

I smiled nervously and turned to Toya. "Thank you for looking out for me. I couldn't ask for a better friend and sister. Please be careful out there and keep in touch with me. I'd die if something happened to you, Toya," I cried and we embraced.

"I'll be okay. Just focus on what we talked about. I got everything handled until you get out. No worries. Okay?" Toya said and wiped my tears.

I nodded and told the nurse that I was ready. As the nurse and I walked away, I turned around one last time and told Toya that I loved her once more. "I love you too, sis. Make me proud," she said and walked out of the facility.

The first week in rehab was really tough on me physically and emotionally. Detox was no joke at all. After that it got a little easier day-by-day. A lot of support groups, meetings with a shrink, writing poetry, and I even started writing a book—all this to keep my mind busy. I am so thankful that Toya didn't kill me after finding out about Angelo and I. She showed me how much she truly loved me when she decided to get me help. She didn't have to do it, but she did. I always said that I would die for her, but now I owe her my life. I just have to focus on getting well like she had told me, so that I can get back out there to help her. I know she needs me; she's just too proud to admit it. When I get out of here I'm going to hunt Angelo down. I've got something special planned for him.

CHAPTER 31

Trey

It's been over a week and I was able to identify our John Doe as Marques, thanks to a missing person report made back in Harford County some months ago. The icing on the cake is that I was able to gather enough evidence to pin the murder on Alberto Hernandez. Everyone at the office was surprised that I was able to solve the case. They had no idea about the information that Sonya had given me. The mayor was pleased and I was rewarded with a promotion.

Meanwhile, I'm still doing my dirt in the streets and making more money than I can count. Toya put me in charge of the strip club, Corey and Nico are now running Park Heights, Booker and Fred were now running Woodlawn, and two of our corner boys were promoted to Booker and Fred's old positions. Toya came home and everything began to run smoothly once again.

Angelo was still on the loose, but no one has heard anything. I'm sure he's somewhere out there regrouping. Toya is far from dumb and didn't become the queen pin because of her looks. She's out there following his trail, ready to hit him while he's still weak. Gutta told us about his little phone call from Angelo, which only tells us what we already know. Angelo is desperate and there is only one place he would go at a time like this, Harford County.

***

Angelo

I've been here for over a week and I can't seem to find any of my old friends. Everyone is either dead or locked up. Looks like things are going to be a little more complicated than I thought. I know for damn sure that I can't last another week staying with my sister. If I wanted a bitch to nag me to death, I'd get married. Plus she's been spending money faster than I can make it.

"Why are you packing? Headed back to the city?" Bernadette asks.

"No. I'm getting a room at the Sheraton," I reply. "Well, damn. Is my house not up to your standards?" she asked, offended.

"Your house is fine, sis. I just need my own space and privacy." I kiss her on the forehead and grab my bags.

"Well, are you still going to help me with the bills? I can't afford them on my own. I just need to last long enough to go to Marques's funeral then I'm moving," she tells me.

"Yeah, I got you. Just send me a screenshot of the bills through text message and I'll handle the rest," I tell her as we walk down stairs.

I spent the rest of the day in my hotel room plotting on how to take down Toya. After numerous phone calls, I finally got in touch with one of my old running buddies. "Who this?" she answered.

"It's Angelo. Miss me?" I ask her.

"Angelo? When did your ass get out? I heard you were out, but I didn't believe it because you hadn't called me. I thought for sure that I would have been one of the first people you'd call," she said with much attitude.

"My bad, Rhonda. I've been busy with handling business. You know how it is." I laugh.

"Yeah, yeah, yeah. Whatever, nigga! I moved to Edgewater Village in Edgewood. You coming by?" she asked.

"Just text me the address and I'll be there within an hour," I tell her.

"Aight, I'll see you soon then." She hangs up.

Rhonda was my first childhood crush. We grew up next door to each other and our moms were good friends as well. She was the true definition of a tomboy. Soon my crush faded and we became the best of friends. She played ball with my brothers and I, fought with us, ran the streets with us, and even sold dope for us. I think the song "Rhonda" by Pastor Troy was written about her. She was a thug to the tenth power.

Before heading out to Edgewood, I lined up my goatee and took a shower. After getting dressed, I went straight to my car and drove down Route 40 towards Edgewood. Man I remember when there used to be a Sizzlers right here, I thought to myself. Driving through Edgewood brought back a ton of memories. My high school and Edgewood High were rivals, especially in basketball. Guaranteed you were going to see a lot of fights when Aberdeen and Edgewood played against each other.

When I arrived at Rhonda's apartment building, I walked past a group of females talking in the stairwell. All four of them were fine as hell, but one of them stood out the most. She was a stallion, stacked in all the right places. Just the sight of her made my dick rock hard. I wink at her and walk upstairs to Rhonda's apartment.

When I knocked on the door, the stallion from downstairs shouted, "Who you looking for?" she asked.

"I'm looking for Rhonda," I shouted back.

"She's not there, boo," she tells me. "You know where I can find her? I'm supposed to be meeting her here," I reply.

"I'm right here, Angelo." She laughed.

Hold up, that stallion downstairs can't be Rhonda! The Rhonda I knew was a tomboy and the woman downstairs is far from that. I jog back downstairs and approach her. "You can't be Rhonda. The Rhonda I know would have cornrows in her hair, some sweatpants, and a tee shirt on, and a pair of tennis shoes," I say to her.

She laughs. "Boy, stop playing. You're bringing back some old memories. I'm all grown up now," she tells me and gives me a hug. "Aight, girls. I'll talk to y'all later. I have to chop it up with an old friend," she tells her three friends.

They all say their goodbyes and walk towards another apartment building.

Rhonda and I went into her place and caught up with each other. We talked about old times and what we were up to nowadays. We ordered Chinese, drank wine, and spent the whole night talking. By three in the morning, I had told her about everything that was going on back in Baltimore.

"I see. So you're here for me to help?" she asks.

"Basically," I tell her.

"I can do that, but what's in it for me?" Rhonda asks.

"You'll be second in charge once I get my empire back. You'll make more money than you can count," I tell her.

Rhonda sits back on the couch and thinks about my offer. She sits back up and places her wine glass on the table. "Okay, I'll help. There's just one condition. We do this my way. You and I have to be on the same page at all times and there are no secrets between us. I have to be able to trust you," she says.

"I wouldn't have it any other way," I tell her and we shake hands.

"Good. Now, I got some phone calls to make. You can go back to your room and I'll have you an army by tomorrow afternoon," Rhonda says and stands up.

I get off the couch and give her a hug. "Thanks, ma. You won't regret this."I left Rhonda that morning, knowing that I made a great choice.

Around two that afternoon Rhonda called me and told me to meet her back at her place. I dragged myself out of bed, took a shower, and brushed my teeth. There was a knock on my door. "Room service!"

It was housekeeping. I opened the door and let her into the room. "I just need some fresh towels, soap, and the bed made," I tell her and hand her a ten-dollar bill.

"Yes, Mr. Wettles. Thank you," she tells me and I leave.

When I made it back to Rhonda's apartment I was greeted by a room full of old and new faces. She must have called all of my old crew and they brought their friends as well. Rhonda walked me around the living room and introduced me to all of the people I didn't know. They knew me and my reputation, but I never met them before. I caught up with my old crew and found out that there were even more people that I had to meet, but couldn't make it today. I knew Rhonda would come through for me, but this was much more than I had expected. Now I have to hatch up a plan on taking down Toya and her crew.

CHAPTER 32

Toya

It's been weeks since anyone has seen or heard from Angelo. Word back home was that he had teamed up with some bitch named Rhonda. I hope he wasn't dumb enough to think that word wouldn't get back to me. Every move he made in Harford County was being reported back to me. I have eyes and ears everywhere. Supposedly this Rhonda chick is official and not to be taken lightly. That just means that I'll enjoy killing her publicly, just to show these fools that I'm the one and only H.B.I.C. out here. Trey is doing his thing with the strip club and even found him a woman to settle down with. Clyde says business is booming back in Louisiana and Angela even thanked me for helping her with Mookie. Things couldn't be running any better for me. All I have to do is remove this thorn in my side, Angelo and now Rhonda.

"Please sign in ma'am," the receptionists tell me.

I sign my name on to the visitors' list and have a seat in the lobby. Sonya walked in and smiled from ear to ear when she saw me. "Hey girl!" she said and hugged me.

"You look great. How are things going?" I asked her.

"I feel like a brand new person. Still taking things one day at a time and they offered me a job here once I'm done with my recovery," she smiled with pride.

"That's great! I'm so happy for you. I knew you could do it," I said.

Sonya and I talked for the duration of my visitation, but I didn't tell her about anything that was going on with business. I didn't want to tempt her into leaving early. I've even thought about keeping her away from the business when she got out of rehab. It's great that they offered her a job. Overall, the choice will be hers to make when she gets out.

After leaving the rehab facility, I called Clyde, but he didn't answer my call. I sent him a text for him to call me when he was free. I figured that I might as well check on all my spots in the meantime. First I stopped by Park Heights to see how things were running. I love doing pop up visits on my workers. They can't hide anything from me if they don't know that I'm coming. I was impressed with how organized Corey and Nico were. They had everything moving like clock work and even beefed up security. Booker and Fred were doing a great job with Woodlawn as well. I let both locations know that I had to make a trip out to New York in the next two days and that if they had any problems to call me or Trey. I had some business to handle with my connect and he never talks business over the phone.

I spent the rest of the day at Sonya's condo, relaxing, and reading a book by one of my favorite authors, K'wan, with a glass of wine. Two hours into the book, my phone beeps, indicating that I had a text message. It was Clyde telling me that he was sorry that he had missed my call and that he would call me first thing tomorrow morning. I poured myself another glass of wine and continued to read my book until I could hardly keep my eyes open. I forced myself off of the recliner and went to the bathroom to take a shower then called it a night.

***

Clyde

I swear I tried to be a good boy while Toya was out of town, but a man has needs. I fucked around and got drunk at the club. I woke up the next morning next to some bitch from the night before and felt guilty as hell for it. No more drinking unless it's in the privacy of my own home. You would think that what happened to Michelle would scare me straight. I really think I have a problem with flirting with bitches and fucking around with them. I need to get my shit straight before Toya comes back or I will end up floating in the Red River.

I woke up whatever her name is from the club and sent her on her way by lying about having an appointment. After she left, I took a shower, got dressed, and headed out to the traps that Toya had set up around town. The first location she opened up was a weed spot on Lacassine. Some of the neighborhood dope boys ran it for her and turned out to be real go-getters and very loyal. Toya always paid her workers well and in return they gave her their loyalty. Plus the reputation she made for herself in the short time she was here put fear in the hearts of the most hardened goons in Rapides Parish.

Toya had a second spot in lower third that had the best heroin and crack in town. It's crazy how many niggas are on that shit. I've seen some niggas that I went to school with come through to buy. Toya remembered about all of the goons that I told her about during her tour of Alexandria when she had first arrived. They jumped at the chance of making big money. I must say, she is a fucking genius and has the memory of an elephant. Our third spot is on the North Side; they specialize in E pills and white girl or cocaine. Our pain pills and syrup is located off of Lee Street, which is the biggest moneymaker out of all the locations. Toya figured the best place for meth would be in Pineville, Ball, and Tioga. We had the same system running in Marksville as well. I knew Toya was big in the drug game back in Baltimore, but I never would have thought that she could pull all of this off on her own. So much money was coming in so fast that she had to open up a cash house for the money at an undisclosed location before she left. I'm the only person that knows about it, so I have to do all of the pick-ups around town and Marksville. I can't complain because it's money and plenty of it.

Word around town was that Toya was some kind of myth because not too many people have seen her in person. After her little killing spree, she went underground. Only the high-ranking workers knew that she was real. Everyone else only heard stories about the queen pin that kills for fun. Toya prefers that I be in the spotlight instead of her. I love the attention around town. People break their necks just to speak or be seen with me. I'm like a ghetto celebrity and the bitches love it. I had bitches jocking me before the money, but now all kinds of hoes are coming at me now that this money is rolling in. I know they don't really give a fuck about me, because when I had nothing, most of these hoes didn't want to get at a nigga. Toya is the only girl that has ever given a damn about me and put money in my pockets. That's why she is and will always be wifey.

CHAPTER 33

Rhonda

I'm glad that Angelo came to me for help. I've been waiting for the chance to get back at Toya for a long ass time. I have my own personal reasons for teaming up with Angelo. That's why I made it very clear that we do things my way. Growing up with Angelo and Tek taught me a lot of valuable lessons; I learned what to do and what not to do. I was a little older than Tek and younger than Angelo, kind of stuck in the middle. They treated me like a sister and showed me so many things dealing with the drug game. Of course when Angelo was locked up the crown was handed to Tek and I was forgotten about. That was until I bloomed into a beautiful young woman and Tek took notice of me. He and I rekindled our friendship and eventually it grew into something more serious. That was until Toya came into the picture and swooped him up. Tek only came around when Toya was out of town and he needed a nut. Eventually Toya killed him and a piece of me died with him.

Now here I am, sitting on my couch, drinking some wine and plotting on the best revenge known to mankind. Toya took away someone that I loved and in return I will do the same to her. Now that I have Angelo in my back pocket, I have one more person to add into the equation. There is no way that Toya will be able to take on all three of us. If by chance she does come out of this unscathed, then, and only then, will I bow down. My first mission is to go to Bmore and do some research on Toya and everyone around her. I'm going to hit her where it hurts the most, her pockets and her heart. It's finally my time to shine and nobody, not even Angelo better get in my way.

***

Trey

My life has been much more pleasant ever since Toya has been back home. Running the strip club has been enjoyable and I even met a good woman. The first time I came into the club Joy caught my eye. She's not a dancer, just the manager and bartender. She and I have talked over drinks at the bar. Joy doesn't drink but she'd sit and listen, as I'd have a drink or two while telling her about the drama in my life, minus the illegal shit. When I finally ran out of things to talk about, she surprised me with her story. Not only does she go to college, but also she has a second job at a law firm as a paralegal.

"My mom would love you," I tell her.

"Well, I'm sure that I would love her too," Joy replied.

"So how about you and I go by her house some time this week," I suggest.

"I would love to meet your mom." She smiled.

A week later, Joy and I went to my mom's house for dinner.

"Ms. Cummings, I've heard so much about you. It's nice to finally meet you," Joy said and held her hand out for a handshake.

"Nice to meet you too baby, but we give hugs around here," my mom said and hugged Joy. I was pleased that they were getting along so soon. "Y'all come on in and have a seat. I cooked something special for dinner." Mom smiled and escorted us in.

Joy and mom talked the whole time as if I wasn't there. They hit it off as if they'd known each other for years. Mom was telling her all of my embarrassing moments as a child and Joy was telling my mom about her family, schooling, and jobs. My mom went all out for dinner. She cooked some cabbage, fried chicken, baked mac and cheese, black-eyed peas, hot water corn bread, and peach cobbler for dessert.

"Think you cooked enough, Ma?" I laughed.

"Baby, you know I was going to cook up a storm when you told me that you were finally bringing a girl to meet me," she replied.

After dinner, Joy helped my mom with clearing off the table and washing the dishes. Afterwards they had a cup of coffee with dessert.

"So, Trey and I are opening up a soul food place here in Baltimore. What do you think about that?" Mom asked Joy.

"I think that's a great idea. I know for a fact that your cooking will bring in a lot of customers," she replied.

The announcement caught me off guard. "You really mean that, Ma?" I asked.

My mom nodded and smiled.

"I'll start looking at some properties this week," I tell her.

"You go on and do that son. I trust your judgment," she said.

We talked about the business for a little while longer before Joy and I decided to call it a night. I kissed and hugged my mom good night and told her that I would be back later on that week.

"I really enjoyed spending time with your mom. She's very sweet and the food was amazing," Joy said as I walked her to the front door of her home.

"I can tell that she enjoyed your company as well. Thanks for coming with me," I said and kissed her on the cheek. We said our good nights and I headed home for another long night in homicide. Today was definitely a good day. My mom is happy, Joy is happy, and I'm happy that they are happy.

CHAPTER 34

Angelo

Now that I have a team ready to go to war for me, I figured it was safe to return back to Bmore. Rhonda decided to stay back in Harford County for two more days to prepare for the take over. I don't mind her staying behind because I need some time to prepare things on my end too. I spent the next two days buying burners and ammo. By the time Rhonda came to Bmore, I had everything set up.

"Are you staying with me or in a hotel?" I asked.

"Didn't you say that Sonya knows where you live? If so, I think it's best that I stay in a hotel. I don't want them knowing that I'm here," Rhonda replied. She had a valid point about Sonya knowing where I live. I never thought about her and Toya coming back to my house to take me out.

"Good idea. I might have to stay at a hotel as well," I said. That evening Rhonda and I check into two separate hotels and then went straight to work.

Rhonda trailed Toya, which turned out to be a little more difficult than she originally thought. I trailed Trey to his night job at the homicide department. I figured I'd call it a night when he didn't come out of the building for the rest of the night.

"Hello?" Rhonda answered the phone.

"I'm going to my room. Not much to see here, because he's at work. I'll finish this tomorrow," I tell her.

"Yeah, I know what you mean. Toya isn't doing shit either. It's almost like they know that we're watching them." She laughs.

Rhonda must be reading my mind because I was thinking the same thing. I hope we don't have a mole in our crew.

"Well, I did get a little bit of information from one of my boys," Rhonda says.

"What did he tell you?" I asked.

"Let me make sure it's legit before I tell you what it is," she says. I felt some type of way because she wouldn't tell me what she knew.

I went to my room and slept until twelve noon. "Damn! I overslept," I said to myself. Before getting in the shower, I turned on the news and made myself a cup of coffee. The local news was reporting on a homicide that took place earlier this morning around two; it was a drug bust and something about the mayor cracking down on violence in the city. After my coffee, I took a shower and brushed my teeth. I dressed comfortably in some jeans, a thermal, Timberlands, and a skully cap. I know where Trey lives so I'm not in a rush to find him. I call up Rhonda to see if she wants to join me for breakfast.

"Good morning. I was calling to see if you wanted to join me for breakfast, but it sounds like you're still sleeping," I tell her.

"I had a long night. I didn't get in until four in the morning," she tells me.

"Four? Why so late? You said you were headed to your room when I had spoke to you last night," I said.

"Yeah, well I had to follow a lead from one of my boys and it turned out to be some very valuable information." She yawns.

After three minutes of trying to convince her to tell me what it was over the phone, she decided to get out of bed so that she can meet me for breakfast to discuss what it was that she had heard.

"I'll meet you in an hour," she says and hangs up.

The suspense was killing me. It must have been something really good. I spent two hours at a local diner, nursing a cup of lemonade, waiting on Rhonda. Finally she arrived looking like she had just stepped out of a magazine. She is fine as hell and I could see us doing some really nasty things together, but I don't want to complicate our partnership.

"You said an hour," I say as I stand up to pull her chair out for her.

"My bad. I can't just come out in public looking like, who done it and why," she smiles. "So what did you find out?" I get straight to the point.

"Alright, so this is what happened..."

***

Trey

I spent a few hours at work, filling out paperwork and doing some research when Detective Flemmings and I received a call about a homicide that had taken place. "Looks like it's going to be another long night," Flemmings says.

I ignore his complaining and gather my things. I prefer being out in the field, rather then sitting behind the desk all damn night. When we arrived at the crime scene, Flemmings went inside the abandoned row home while I got a report from the first responders. Before I could make it inside the house, Flemmings came out and pushed me away from the entrance.

"You need to stay out here, partner," he said.

"What do you mean? Stay out here for what? Move out my way, Flemmings. I have a job to do," I tell him.

"Cummings, please. Just stay out here for me. You don't need to see this," he says with worry in his eyes.

Okay, something is definitely wrong. What doesn't he want me to see?

"What's going on?" I ask him.

"There's too much going on in there. The less people in there, the better. I don't need anyone contaminating the crime scene," Flemmings says and walks away.

Being that he's the lead detective, I take his word for it and look around the premises for signs of what may have occurred. I spent countless hours interviewing witnesses that really didn't see much or didn't want to say anything at all.

"I'm not a snitch" is what most of them said. I was beginning to get frustrated and suspicious. Why am I not allowed inside? I pushed past Flemmings and walked inside the abandoned home. The place was a bloody mess. The victim lay on the ground with a sheet covering her. The police officer outside did say that it was a woman, but her head was missing.

"Did she have any identification on her?" I asked Flemmings.

"We found a locket laying on the ground, next to the body. That's all I can tell you right now," he replied.

"What are you trying to hide?" I asked him.

Flemmings shook his head and walked away. Okay, what the fuck is going on? I'm trying to do my job, but I can't get the job done if people keep hiding shit from me. I approach one of the officers outside and ask him for the locket that was found inside.

"I don't have the locket, sir. You might want to check with the other detective," she says.

I already had it set in my mind that I would have to fight Flemmings tooth and nail for that locket. "Flemmings! I need that locket!" I call out to him.

He acts as though he didn't hear me. When I walk up to him, he continues to jot something down.

"I need to see the locket. How can I do my job properly if you are hiding evidence from me? What kind of partner does that?" I ask him.

"One that cares. Trust me, Cummings. You don't need to see this right now," he said. "Look, I don't care what's going on. I just need to see the evidence," I tell him.

Flemmings stops writing and looks up at me. "I need you to have a seat, buddy. I'm going to hand you this locket, but you need to stay calm," he says and hands me a bag containing the locket.

It looks familiar, but I can't seem to remember where I'd seen it before. I open up the locket and stare at the two pictures inside. The room begins to close in on me and my head is spinning. Please say it ain't so! I rush over to the body and uncover it.

"No! It can't be! How?" I scream. I begin to boil over with rage. Falling over with tears pouring out my eyes, I scream, "I'm gonna kill that nigga!"

CHAPTER 35

Toya

I woke up to someone banging on the door at six this morning. I was having another one of my nightmares, except this time everyone I had killed was chasing me. It seemed like I couldn't run fast enough, like my feet were sinking in glue. I haven't slept well in weeks and it was starting to show in my eyes.

"Hold on!" I yell towards the door.

"Open the door, Toya! Hurry up!" Trey shouts back.

The sound of his voice puts me into high gear. I run to the bathroom to put on a robe and head straight to the door. "Why are you knocking on the door like...?" I stop mid-sentence when I see the look on his face.

Trey rushes into the house and falls to his knees. "What's wrong, bro?" I ask him as I get on the floor with him.

He cried and rocked back and forth, just like he used to do when we were little. His face is twisted with anger and sadness. All I can do is hold him and wait for him to calm down. "Imma kill him, Toya! Imma kill him!" Trey screamed.

"Kill who? What happened? What's wrong?" I ask Trey.

"Angelo happened! She's dead and I should have been there to protect her! It's my fault, sis!" he continues to cry.

I get up and walk to the bathroom to grab some tissue for him. When I get back in the living room, Trey is still on the floor staring blankly at the wall. I know that look all too well. Not too often did Trey get like this, but that blank look means that someone is in grave danger. People thought I was ruthless, and that I was the cold-hearted one. They have no idea how cold Trey can be when pushed to his boiling point. I kneel in front of him and hand him the tissue. Trey pushes my hand away and stands up, wiping his face with the back of his hand. "Momma is dead," he mumbles.

"WHAT?!" I scream.

"Momma is dead, Toya!" Trey shouts at me and grabs me by the shoulders. My mom wasn't perfect. She had her demons, but in the end she cleaned up and made up for all the wrong she had done. I love my mom regardless of what she's done. Someone crossed the line when they killed her. Civilians are suppose to be off limits! This has gone from business to personal and whoever killed my mom better hope that Trey and I never find him.

"Do you know who did it?" I ask Trey.

He shakes his head. "If I knew, I wouldn't be here. I'd be torturing whoever did it," Trey says.

I nod my head and begin to come up with a plan. "Put the word out that whoever comes with information on who did this will get half a million dollars. No questions asked; I just need a name!" I tell him.

Trey turns and walks out the condo on a mission. I hurried into the room and put on some tight jeans, a pink and cream sweater, and some Timberlands. I threw my hair into a ponytail, put on some hoops and go into Sonya's closet to retrieve one of her desert eagles. Before leaving, I made a call to Buck and told him about the situation and what I needed done.

"I'll have that info for you by the end of the day," he says and hangs up. I know that Buck meant what he said. He never made promises that he couldn't keep.

I spent the day at my mom's house, going through her things. Maybe there is a clue in here to let me know who had it out for my mom or what may have happened. From the looks of things, it looks as though she was grabbed out of bed. The room was ransacked; the bed was a mess with traces of blood. There was definitely a struggle in here. I call Trey to tell him what I found and he rushes over to take a look. He immediately puts his detective skills to work.

"Don't touch anything else," he says. "They forced their way into the house. Look at the door and the different footprints on the floor. It was more than one person," he pointed out.

"Are you going to report this back to your job?" I asked.

He shook his head. "Nah, I was taken off of the case. Conflict of interest they say. Fuck 'em. Let them figure it out on their own. I'm not trying to arrest anyone. I'm going to kill the muthafuckas that did this to Ma," he says and walks out of the house.

I follow behind him and ask him some more questions about what he knows.

"I was called in for a body found in an abandoned row home. They wouldn't let me go in at first. Supposedly they found a locket with two pictures in it. The pictures were of you and I." Trey shakes his head.

"I'm scared to ask this question, but I have to know. What did they do to mom?" I ask him.

Trey sheds a tear. "It's fucked up, sis. She was beaten, tortured, and her head was missing. They did her dirty!" he shouts in anger.

I begin to feel hot and my hands start to shake. "I gotta go. Make sure you find a way to lock up mom's house so no one can come in here and take her shit." I hug Trey and run to my car.

I went to all of my trap houses in the city and spread the word to all of my workers. Next, I went to my strip club and held a meeting with Joy and my bouncers. I told them about the cash reward and to spread the word amongst the dancers. I even called Jessup and told him to get the word out in Harford County. At exactly eleven in the evening, Buck calls me.

"You might want to sit down for this," he tells me.

"Just spit it out," I tell him.

"Do you know anyone by the name of..."

***

Rhonda

"Okay, so this is what happened. When I got off the phone with you last night a friend of mine put a little bug in my ear. She told me where I could find Toya's mom," I tell Angelo.

He stops eating and places his fork down on the table. He clears his throat. "What you say?"

I smile at him and nod my head.

"Please tell me you didn't do what I think you did," Angelo pleads with his eyes.

"Give me one good reason on why I shouldn't have. Eye for an eye; she took Tek and I took her mom. Seems like an even exchange to me," I tell him.

Angelo starts to rub his temples. "She was a civilian. People that aren't in the game and haven't done anything to us are off limits!" he explains.

I begin to laugh. "You can't be serious. This bitch killed your little brother and you're worried about some old crack head bitch?" I ask him.

"Damn, Rhonda you fucked up big time. That's unnecessary heat on our backs by the police. Why didn't you talk to me about this before offing the bitch?" Angelo whispers with anger.

"I don't have to explain shit to you! We made a deal that I would do things MY way. Remember that? So you do whatever it is that you do. Which hasn't worked so far, might I add. And I'll do what the fuck I do and that is getting results. I'm here to handle shit the way it should have been handled a long time ago," I say and stand up to leave.Angelo shakes is head in disappointment and all I could do was smile and walk out. One of these days he's going to thank me.

I had a hard time trying to track down Toya. When I made it to the condo that she was staying at, I noticed that her car was already gone. So I just parked and sat there for hours before I decided to call it a night. When I went back to my room that evening, the desk clerk told me that he had a message for me. He handed me a slip of paper that said:

I know you did it and if you want it to remain a secret, you will meet me in the hotel lobby at ten this evening.

So now someone wants to blackmail me. This mystery person must not know who he or she is fucking with.

I look at my watch; it was thirty minutes until I have to meet back in the lobby. I rush up to my room, change into a pair of sweatpants and a hoodie, and then head back downstairs to the lobby. I make sure that I'm sitting down with my back against the wall and wait. At exactly ten, I see the ugliest man I'd ever seen in my life walk into the hotel, followed by three cock diesel niggas.

He approaches me and says, "Ms. Rhonda, I'm assuming? Thanks for meeting me on such short notice."

I don't bother to shake his hand or speak to him. I'll let him do all the talking and when he's done, I'll tell him to kiss my beautiful black ass. "I can see that you want to get down to business, so here it is. I have some valuable information pertaining to an event that you were involved in last night. A client of mine is hell bent on getting revenge on you and whomever else may have helped you. Are you following me?" he says.

I continue to sit and stare a hole into his ugly face.

"I would tell you my name, but I'm pretty sure that you already know who I am. My reputation throughout the whole DMV speaks for itself. So my question to you is, how much is this information worth keeping to myself?" he asks.

I stand up and walk up to him and his three henchmen begin to walk towards me. He raises his hand up and tells them to fall back.

"I don't give a damn if you tell Toya or whoever else about what I did. You'd actually be doing me a favor. I want the bitch to come to me and TRY to do something. You're a dirty ass, good for nothing ass nigga. I don't like that bitch, but you're not loyal. See, I know your type. You're only loyal to dead presidents. Well, I've got news for you, you ugly muthafucka. Not all money is good money. You better watch whose business you're sticking your nose in, 'cause it just might get you killed. Now run back and tell her what the fuck I did and tell her about your sneaky conniving ass ways while you're at it," I tell him and walk off.

That nigga got me fucked up, thinking that I'm going to pay him to keep his mouth shut. Fuck him and the bitch that pushed out his chainsaw massacre looking ass. This nigga got me feeling dirty just by looking at his rancid ass. As soon as I get into my room, I run myself a hot bubble bath to relax. Whoever wants to come for me, can get it.

CHAPTER 36

Clyde

Life couldn't be better for me. I have so much money, that I don't know what to do with it. I decided that the best thing for me to do was to invest it and have a house built on Plantation Road. I figured that Toya would love to live a much larger place. So I bought a lot of land and now a blueprint is being drawn up from my dream home. It will have eight bedrooms, five bathrooms, a theater, large kitchen, living room, den, dining room, man cave, spa, and game room. There will be an indoor pool that starts inside the house and leads outside. The large glass patio doors that surround the pool will be able to slide all the way open for days when the weather is good.

I'm also going to have an outdoor kitchen, but instead of a stove and oven, it'll be a huge grill that can be used with coal, wood, or propane. I'll have surround sound all around the house and backyard, a seven-car garage that I plan to fill up cars for everyday of the week, and last but not least, I'll have a guesthouse with four bedrooms and three bathrooms with an indoor basketball court next door. I know it'll take years to build, but I know it will be worth the wait. I plan on raising our future children in the best home in Alexandria.

I didn't tell Toya about the house, I want to surprise her when she gets home. By the time she gets back, the house should just be getting started. I haven't heard from her much. I know that she's dealing with a lot, so I give her space. I don't want to add onto her stress, so I just handle business like I'm suppose to and make sure that I put her money in a safety deposit box at the bank.

Even though I'm doing all of these things that most women would love, I still feel like a piece of shit. Why? Well, I can't seem to keep my dick to myself. I really think I'm addicted to pussy. No matter how hard I try, I can't turn away from it. One girl in particular has got my nose wide open. I don't love her, but the sex is amazing. She's the closest that I can get to Toya. I don't think that I'll ever find someone as good in bed as Toya. Maybe that's my problem. I'm searching for that feeling to fill the void that Toya left. I know she's coming back, but until then, I need to fuck bitches. I know I'm wrong and I know the consequences that I would have to face if Toya were to ever find out, which is why I know that I have a problem. Maybe I need to get some help.

***

Bernadette

Marques's funeral has came and gone. Word around town is that my brother had something to do with his murder. I don't want to believe that my brother would be so cold-hearted that he would kill the father of his nephew. Deep down inside, I know that he is capable of doing anything. What can I do? I'm torn between my flesh and blood and the love of my life. Did my brother give a damn about how I would feel about him killing my son's father? Obviously, he didn't give a damn about my feelings. So why should I care about his well being? I should call the Baltimore Police Department and tell them everything that I know about Angelo. Then I should call his parole officer as well. The little bit of love that I had left for my brother is now gone. I hate him with a passion and hope to God that he gets what is coming to him. Karma is my best friend and that bitch always comes around.

I decided that I would send M.J. to Queens, New York with my aunt while I prepared for our move to Columbus, Georgia. I didn't want to let him go, but it had to be done. Some of my church family helped me box up things and put them in storage until I was ready to come back and get them. My pastor and church even put together money to help me with my new beginning. Marques didn't have life insurance so they also helped with paying for his head stone. I'm sure going to miss Maryland. I have a lot of good memories here, but I need a change. Before heading to New York to spend a week with family and getting M.J., I visit my pastor and his wife.

"So, how do you feel about this move?" pastor asked.

"It's bittersweet. I don't want to leave, but I have to. I need this new job and M.J. deserves a new start," I tell him.

"You do what you have to do for your son, honey. You're a good mother and don't you ever forget that," the first lady tells me.

I nod my head and hug the both of them. "I'll be back in a few months to get the last of my things out of storage," I tell them.

"Make sure you come see us. Keep in touch and don't ever hesitate to call us, you hear?" the pastor said.

"Yes, sir. I'll definitely keep in touch. Thanks for everything, pastor," I tell him and walk to my car.

As I head onto I-95, I shed a few tears. "I'm going to miss you Aberdeen; you will always be my home. Thank you for the memories, good and bad."

CHAPTER 37

Toya

After getting off the phone with Buck, I called Trey to let him know what I was told. "What's up?" he asks.

"Buck just called me with some information, but I'm even more confused. Maybe you can help me figure this out," I tell him.

"Alright, what did he say?" Trey asks.

"Supposedly some bitch named Rhonda and some niggas had something to do with mom's murder. Do you know anyone by that name?" I ask him.

Trey takes a moment to answer. "It doesn't ring a bell. So you're telling me that someone we don't know killed mom? That makes no sense. Maybe it's someone that she knew. That doesn't answer the question on why someone wanted mom dead. She didn't have anything worth taking. Nothing was taken out of the house and her locket was left behind," he says.

Everything Trey is saying makes sense. "Buck told me what she looks like, but she still doesn't sound familiar. I guess we will have to dig around some more. Until then, watch your back, bro," I tell him and hang up.

It's been two months since I got that information from Buck and I still haven't figured out who Rhonda is. Buck even tried setting up a meeting with her last month, but she never showed. Instead, my trap house in Park Heights was burned down. I lost a lot of money, including everyone in there. Whoever lit the fire made sure that there was no way in or out of there. I'm far from stupid. I know that this Rhonda bitch had something to do with it. The exact time and day she was suppose to meet up with Buck, my shit gets burned down. I can't wait to get my hands around her fucking neck! Angelo has been incognito, but I know he's out there. Something tells me that Rhonda and Angelo might be working together. If I'm right, I need to find Angelo and bring this shit to an end. I'm tired of this cat and mouse bullshit. Somebody's gotta die and it won't be me!

Unfortunately, I'll never have the honor of killing Angelo. The mayor started something called operation clean up. Too many murders and crimes are taking place in abandoned homes, so the city is either knocking them down or fixing them up for low-income families. While going through one of the boarded up homes, a city employee found Angelo's body with a gunshot to the head. I wonder who did it and how they were able to get close enough to shoot him at point blank range. Maybe it was that bitch Rhonda. I wish I could say that my problems are over, but they aren't. Rhonda is still out here lurking in the shadows. Sonya is finally done with rehab and back in the business. She decided not to take the job that they had offered her which is fine by me, because I could really use her help. With Trey, Sonya, and I back together, we are unstoppable.

***

Sonya

Toya welcomed me home with a surprise party and a bunch of cash. It felt good to be back home with the ones I love. I was even told that Angelo was dead, which made my day that much better. Of course I wanted to kill him for what he had done to me, but that fact that he's dead is okay with me. I got back into the swing of things after Toya updated me on everything that's been going on. I can't believe that we lost Park Heights to a fire. Thank God Trey no longer worked the traps; we could have lost him as well. My main focus is going to be on finding out who Rhonda is. She opened up Pandora's Box when she killed Ms. Cummings. I owe Toya my life. She could have given up on me, but she got me help instead and I could never repay her for what she's done for me. In return, I will find Rhonda and deliver her to Toya with a red bow.

Trey was dating Joy when I got out, but all of that changed when I touched down. I can't deny that the love was always there, but we never crossed that line until now. Trey told me about how he felt about me, which surprised me because I never noticed. After our long talk, the relationship took on a whole new meaning; I am his Bonnie and he is my Clyde. Toya moved into Trey's place and Trey moved in with me. I feel like I'm in a dream that I don't want to wake up from. Trey treats me like a queen. I want for nothing and in return I treat him like a king.

One night Trey and I were on our way out to dinner. We stopped at a red light and I just happened to look at the car next to us. There were two females in there. The one in the driver's seat was deformed as if she had been in a bad accident. I didn't get a good look at the one in the passenger seat. The driver looked back me and gave me the most disturbing smile I'd ever seen. Something about her seemed familiar, like I've seen her before. The light turned green and the car sped off.

"Hmm, that was weird," I say out loud.

"What's weird?" Trey asks.

"Nothing, boo. Just thought I saw someone that I knew," I tell him.

Trey and I enjoyed our meals and laughed about our childhood. He made fun of how I would sneak food out of the house, thinking my mom didn't notice. "You really looked out for us, Sonya. Our childhood would have turned out much different if Toya had never met you," Trey tells me.

I blush and grab ahold of his hand. "Your sister did just as much for me. She looked out for me in school. No one dared to fuck with me." I laughed.

After eating, Trey and I weren't ready to leave, so he had another glass of wine while I sipped on a coke. "I have something that I need to talk to you about," I tell him.

"Sure, what is it?" he asks.

I reach into my purse and pull out a pacifier. I hand it to him and he twists up his face in confusion. "What am I suppose to do with this?" he asks.

"Babies use those, duh!" I tell him.

His eyes grow wide and his smile even wider. "You mean?" Trey asks.

I nod my head and begin to laugh. "Oh, shit! Imma be a daddy? Yo! Imma be a daddy!" he shouts.

Everyone turned and looked at him like he had lost his damn mind. I'm just happy that he took the news so well. I was kind of worried that he would say that he wasn't ready. He called Toya and told her the good news as we waited for valet to bring our car. As he was talking to her, I noticed that car driving by slowly. The window rolled down and that;s when I got a better look at the driver.

It's the bitch that Toya had cut up with a box cutter back in the day! The car comes to a stop in the middle of the street and she exits the car with an AK. I reach behind me for my desert eagle and push Trey behind a car as the bullets start flying. I let my gun bark and I run for cover. I can hear the bullets ripping through a few cars and glass shattering. She must have run out of ammo, because the shooting stopped and the sound of a car speeding off could be heard. Car alarms were going off, the sounds of sirens are in the background, and people inside the restaurant are screaming.

The window had been shot out and some of the diners were lying on the ground either dead or wounded. That's when I realized that Trey wasn't moving.

"Trey?!" I scream and I rush to him. "Trey? Baby, get up! Trey!" I scream. I roll him over, looking for blood.

"Somebody help! Oh, God. No! Somebody please help!" I shout.

Trey was shot twice. Once in the shoulder and one in the abdomen. He was losing a lot of blood and I knew that time was of the essence. The ambulance finally came but wouldn't let me ride with them.

"Which hospital are you taking him to?" I ask.

"Johns Hopkins," the EMS tells me.

I hail a cab and tell him to bring to the hospital as fast as possible.

CHAPTER 38

Toya

Trey called me with great news. I'm going to be an auntie and my best friend is the mother. He was ranting and raving about all the things he wanted to get the baby when the phone went dead. "Hello? Trey?"

I look at the screen of my phone to see if the call had ended. Oh, well, I'm sure he'll call me back. Before he had called, I was in his condo cleaning up the mess he had left behind. I swear some men act like cleaning up is a sin. He had dirty clothes all over the floor that took me a few hours to clean, dry, fold, and put away. I can't be mad at him; he had been pretty busy. As I was ironing his shirts, my phone rang. It's Sonya.

"Hey, girl! Congrats..." I was talking when she cut me off.

"Toya! Get to Johns Hopkins now! It's Trey, he..." I didn't give her a chance to finish what she was saying. The words Johns Hopkins and Trey made me hang up and rush out the door. I don't know how fast I was driving, but I know that I was driving like a mad woman, weaving in and out of traffic.

When I got to the hospital, I ran in and asked a lady at the counter where I could find Trey Cummings. Before she could answer me, I saw Sonya speed walking towards me. "This way!"

She grabs my hand and leads me to the elevator. "He's in surgery right now," she tells me. Her eyes were red and puffy from crying.

"Tell me what the fuck happened!" I shout.

Sonya tells me in detail about the ride to dinner, and when they were leaving. "So that's why his call dropped with me. I was wondering why he hadn't called back. Why are you just now calling me? This was hours ago!" I tell her.

Sonya shakes her head. "With all the chaos? I was in shock!" she explains.

Before I could get any more information from her, the doctor walks up to us.

"Are you the family of Mr. Cummings?" he asks.

"Yes, I'm his sister and this is his wife. How is he?" I ask.

"Well, we did all that we could; the rest is up to him. He's in critical condition as of now. He's seems like a fighter, so I have hope that he'll make it through. He lost a lot of blood, so we had to give him a blood transfusion as well. He is in a coma, so right now it is a waiting game," he tells us.

I tell the doctor thank you and begin to fill out some paperwork that a nurse had handed to me.

"It was her. I saw her face, Toya! I didn't want to believe it. I should have known that she was going to do something crazy. It's all my fault! If I had only warned him about it, none of this would have happened," Sonya cries.

I turn to my right to face her. "Stop with all the bullshit and just tell me who you're talking about." I clench my teeth to stop from slapping the piss out of her.

"That girl from Aberdeen! The one you had cut up with the box cutter," she answers.

"That bitch! I should have killed her when I had the chance! This is the second time that she's come after me." I turned a blind eye to what had happened at the mall years back, because I figured I deserved that one. That should have made things even between us, but now she has a death wish and I'm going to be the one to grant it for her.

I was deep in thought when Sonya asks, "Do you think that she might be the one that killed your mom?"

I was thinking the same thing, but I know that there was more than one person involved.

"I think that she had something to do with it," I answer.

"I'm gonna hunt her down!" Sonya screams.

"You'll do no such thing. I want this one and you're pregnant. If something were to happen to you or that baby, Trey would never forgive me and I could never forgive myself," I tell her.

"Let me help you, Toya! She came after me as well. It's only right that I get my hands dirty too," she says. I stand up from my seat and begin to walk away. "Where are you going? I'm coming with you!" Sonya protests.

"I'm just going to change clothes and grab us a bite to eat. Stay here with Trey just in case things change. I need you here," I tell her.

When I get to my brother's place, I notice that the door has been kicked in. I pull one of Sonya's desert eagles out from my purse and walk in quietly. I can hear someone in the back room going through the dresser. As I approach the bedroom door, I can see a shadow moving around the room. I take a deep breath and get into my zone, preparing myself for battle. My tunnel vision kicks in and I enter the room with the gun cocked and ready.

"You better not move a got damn muscle!" I growl. The person stops moving and her hands go up in surrender. "Now turn around slowly and take off the ski mask with one hand!" I instruct. The person does as told and that's when I was faced with a ghost from my past. "So it's you! What makes you think that you can come for me and my family? Who are you working with?" I ask.

Scar Face smiles and laughs. "Bitch, fuck you! I'm not telling you shit!" she says and spits at my feet. All of a sudden, she runs towards me and I catch her in the face with the butt of my gun.

Scar Face falls to the floor and uses her legs to sweep my feet from under me and I go crashing to the floor. The wind gets knocked out of me and I try to regain my composure, when she climbs on top of me and begins to choke me. I try to pry her hands from around my neck, but her grip is too tight. I can see the desert eagle from the corner of my eye, so I try reaching for it. She begins to bang my head on the floor with all of her strength and my vision begins to blur. I continue to try to reach the gun, stretching my arm as far as I can. The room begins to slowly fade as my lungs begin to burn.

That's when I feel the cold metal of the gun against my fingertips. I grip the gun and hit her twice in the temple with the butt of the gun. Scar Face passes out on top of me and I push her off. Turning to my side, I start to cough violently. It takes me a moment to catch my breath. She's out cold, but I don't want to kill her yet. I need to get some information out of her, so I search the condo for something to tie her up with. I find a long extension cord and hog-tie her with it. Afterwards I sat on the bed and waited for her to come to. While waiting, my phone rings.

"Not right now, Sonya," I speak into the phone.

"I'm just checking on you. It's taking you a long time to get back," she says.

"I'm fine. I'll be there in a little while," I tell her. Scar Face starts to move and her eyes flutter open. "I gotta go," I tell Sonya and hang up.

"Welcome back, bitch." I smile. She struggles to move, but to no avail. I stand up and start to kick her wildly. "You... stupid...ugly...bitch! You...gone...learn...today...hoe!" I scream between each kick and stomp.

My right leg gets tired so I switch to the other leg and continue to stomp on her until I grow tired. As she lay there bleeding, I went to the kitchen to find the dullest knife that I can find. When I get back into the room, I kneel down beside her. "We're going to play a little game. I ask a question and you answer, okay?" I ask sweetly.

She tries to spit on me but fails. I laugh at her attempt and punch her in the bridge of her nose. Blood gushes out and trickles down the sides of her face.

"Okay, let's try this again. I will ask a question and you will answer it. If you fail to answer a question, I will use this knife to reopen a scare on your face." I smile and hold up the dull knife for her to see. "Question number one. Who are you working with?" I ask.

"Fuck you!" she screams.

"Wrong answer." I smile and put the knife up to one of her scars. It takes awhile to cut open because the knife is so dull.

She screams in agony, "Aaauugh! You bitch!" This went on for a while before she was finally ready to talk.

I stand up and smile down at my bloody masterpiece. "It's about time, 'cause I was running out of places to cut. You're a tough nut to crack." I laugh.

"It's Rhonda. She killed your mom; I just helped. My beef is with you and the other bitch. I didn't mean to hurt your brother," she cries.

"Well you did, so for that you have to die. Now, who is Rhonda?" I ask.

"She was the other girl from back in the day when you cut me," she mumbled.

She even told me about the offer that Buck made to Rhonda and that Rhonda skipped town for a while until things died down. I should have known that if Scar Face was here, the bitch wasn't too far behind.

"Well, that's the only questions I had. Now, how hard was that?" I ask as I grab the desert eagle from on top of the bed.

"Any last words?" I ask her.

"My daughter; she's only eight years old. I just want her to know..." she began, but I cut her off.

"Hold up, you mean to tell me that someone got your ugly ass pregnant?" I laugh uncontrollably. Scar Face starts to cry and I wipe the tears of laughter off my face. "You fucked with the wrong family. You should have done your research a little more before coming for me. I don't feel sorry for you or your bastard ass kid. I'll see you in hell, bitch," I tell her.

I use her for target practice, shooting her in both legs, then her arms. I always wondered what would happen if I were to shoot a bitch in the pussy, so I answered my question by shooting her in the crotch and lastly, the head. When I was done, I called Buck and told him to meet me at Trey's for a clean up job. Then I called Gutta and told him to come by with some of the corner boys. All that killing made me hungry and horny. My dick is in Louisiana, so I guess I'll just settle for something to eat while I wait for everyone to arrive.

CHAPTER 39

Rhonda

Nicole went crazy and shot at Sonya and Trey in the middle of the street; I knew she was going to do it. I'm the one that came up with the plan. When I saw Sonya at that red light, I knew that we had to take advantage of the opportunity. Afterwards, I had her take me back to the room to pack up my shit. When I was done packing, I checked out of the hotel and went straight to BWI airport. I had to get ghost for a while until the heat died down. I don't know when I'm going back; it might be a week, a month, a year, or maybe even three years. One thing I know for sure is that I am going back and when I do, they won't know what hit them. They killed Angelo and left him to rot in an abandoned building. I knew then that I had to leave. I decided that the best place for me to go was to the Dominican Republic to stay with my mom's side of the family. I need the vacation anyway.

I've been here for two weeks and I feel refreshed. The feel of warm sand between my toes, the sound of waves crashing, and the heat of the sun on my beautiful bronzed skin feels like heaven. I could get used to this way of living. I just might buy a piece of property here and make this my getaway spot. As I'm sitting at the beach, sipping on a pina colada, my phone rings.   "Hello?" I sing into the phone.

"So you skipped town and ran like a little bitch huh?" a voice comes over the phone. I look at the caller I.D. on my screen; it's Nicole's phone number, but it's not her voice. "Who is this?" I ask.

"You know exactly who this is! You killed my mom, got my brother shot up, and leave?" she asks.

"Ahhh! This must be Toya. How is Trey?" I laugh.

"Look, bitch! You can run all you want to, but you will eventually have to come back and when you do...." She stopped talking for a moment. "I'm going to kill you just like I killed your ugly scarred up friend. Bitch, you better hope that I don't find you!" she says and hangs up.

That phone call was rather entertaining. I hope she doesn't think that I'm afraid of her or her little sidekick, Sonya. That's far from the truth. She should know just like I do, that it's best to move in silence. I want her to be on edge until I return. While I'm here on this wonderful island, she's in grimy ass Baltimore watching over her shoulder. Seems to me like I'm the one that's winning. I'm not going to dwell on the bullshit. I'm just going to sit here and enjoy my drink. This drink is for you, Nicole. Rest in peace, boo; you did good!

***

Toya

As I was taking the last bite of my sandwich, there came a knock at the door. I looked through the peephole to see if it was Buck or Gutta and open the door.

"What's good boss lady?" Gutta asked.

"Come in and have a seat," I tell him and his five homies. They walk in and have a seat on the sofa and love seat. "I asked y'all to come here today to help me with a little situation. I'm not going to tell you what it is. I just need all six of you to follow my lead. Understood?" I ask. "Overstood, boss. We got you," Gutta says.

I grab the guys something to drink and make small talk to pass the time. After thirty minutes of waiting, there's another knock at the door. I allow Buck and his brothers entrance into the house and lead Buck to the back room.

"I need this mess cleaned up as if it never happened," I tell him.

"This will cost you fifty thousand," he tells me.

"Whatever. Just clean it up. You know that my money is always good." I smirk and walk off.

When I walked back into the living room, I told Buck's brother that they could join him in the room to help clean up. Gutta had a confused look on his face, but he knew better than to ask me what was going on. Instead of telling Gutta what I wanted, I texted him a message and he nodded his head. I begin to walk back to the room, pulling out the desert eagle from behind me as Gutta and his crew followed close behind. When they saw me draw my gun, they did the same.

Buck and his brothers were so busy with cleaning up, that they didn't notice me and the boys standing behind them.

"So, tell me something, Buck. This ugly bitch that you're disposing of told me that you tried to do some grease ball shit behind my back. You tried to make a deal with Rhonda?" I asked.

Buck and his brothers stopped moving and turned around to face me. "Don't take it personal, doll face. It's business. Money talks and bullshit walks. You know how it is. Charge it to the game." He smirks.

"Get that smug look off your ugly ass face!" I shout at him.

Gutta takes the lead and cold cocks Buck in the face. Buck falls to the ground and his eye begins to swell to the size of a golf ball. His brother didn't dare move because they knew that they were outnumbered.

"Well, you shouldn't take this shit personal either," I tell him. I cock my gun and shoot all three of his brothers between the eyes.

Buck starts to laugh like a maniac. "I been trying to figure out how I was gonna get rid of them. Tired of splitting my money four ways. Bitch, you did me a favor."

I start to laugh with him and he gets quiet. I think it finally hit him that I was far crazier than him. "Split money? You can't split shit or spend shit if you're dead!" I scream and turn him into Swiss cheese, shooting until my clip is empty.

"Boss!" Gutta shouts.

"Huh?" I ask.

"He's dead. Ain't no bullets left in the clip," he whispers to me.

I didn't realize that I was still pulling the trigger far after the clip had emptied.

Gutta and his boys offered to clean up the mess for me, which was great. I just wanted to get a nut. As they cleaned up, Gutta found Scar Face's cell phone and gave it to me.

"This will come in handy, thanks," I tell him and leave him behind to go the bathroom for a long, hot shower.

It's time for me to go back to Louisiana. I know that Trey will be in good hands with Sonya and if things change with his condition, I can always catch a flight back. As far as Rhonda is concerned, I know that bitch won't be back for a pretty long time. If she thinks anything like me, she'll wait until things cool all the way down, regroup, and come back stronger. I'll stick around for three more weeks to make sure that everything is kosher, and then I'm gone.

CHAPTER 40

Sonya

It's been a few weeks and there hasn't been any improvement with Trey. I still talk to him as if he is not in a coma, hoping that he can hear me. Toya hit me with the news that she was going back to Louisiana to handle the business down there. I don't think that it's a good idea that she leaves right now. Trey still needs the both of us here. Not to mention that Rhonda is still on the loose. Not that I'm afraid of her, but I know that Toya wants to handle that personally. I can't make her stay no matter how much I want her to stay. How does she expect me to run the business here and look after Trey? Granted, she did tell Gutta to help me out, but I don't know him like that. I pray that Trey wakes up before the baby comes.

I spent the last few days setting up a new trap to replace the one that was burned down in Park Heights. I can't replace Cook and the loyal workers that I had working there. I gave Gutta the job of finding some more workers that can be trusted. I hate that I can't have my old crew back; we were all close. As the new trap was getting back into the swing of things, Toya and I were able to take a quick trip to Brooklyn before she flew out to Louisiana. I never had the honor of meeting the connect until now. Toya always made the trips by herself in the past. When we got there Beast and Sincere greeted us at a Jamaican restaurant during closed hours. They patted us down and told us to have a seat.

"Don't talk, unless spoken to," Toya tells me. I nod my head and look around nervously.

In walks a man that looks like Shabba Ranks but with dreads that reach down to his butt. Toya introduced us. "Rasta, this is Sonya. The one I've been telling you about," Toya tells him.

He kisses the back of my hand and smiles at me with a mouth full of gold teeth. We spent an hour there and the meeting was over. Come to find out, he doesn't even live in the United States. He flies to New York from either England or Jamaica whenever necessary. Toya made it clear that I am to come to New York at least once a month. Time and dates are supposed to be scheduled through either Beast or Sincere. The very next morning Toya flew back to Louisiana, but made it clear that if there were any changes with Trey that I am to call her.

***

Toya

It was hard to leave Sonya and Trey behind, but money calls and I can't just quit what I had started in Louisiana. I made sure that I showed Sonya all of the ins and outs of the business before I left, giving her the tools and knowledge that she will need to succeed. It's still my empire, but she has to be able to run it the same way that I would. The flight back to Louisiana was peaceful this time. I didn't have to kill anyone, so that's a plus I guess. After retrieving my baggage from baggage claim, I headed to where I had my car parked. I place my luggage in the trunk, got in the car, and set my GPS to Clyde's address.

Before pulling off I tried to call him to let him know that I was on my way. When he didn't answer, I stopped by a gas station with a bathroom to change my clothes. I went through my bags in the trunk and picked out a tan trench coat, a sexy all white lace panty set, and some red stilettos. I figured I would put them on and surprise him at home.

After the long drive there, I made sure to turn off my headlights before pulling into the driveway. The house was dark; it seemed like he wasn't even there. I left my bags in the trunk and quietly opened the door with my key. The moment I walked in, I could here noise coming from the bedroom. I know he's not doing what I think he's doing! The closer I got to the room, the louder the noise became. There's a bitch in my house, in my bed, with my man. Instead of busting into the room, I went to the kitchen to grab a pair of latex gloves. I took my time putting them on. I'm not in a rush to do what I gotta do. Afterwards I went into his office and unstrapped his gun from under the desk. I made sure that it was fully loaded and cocked it.

Thank God for carpeted floors; they didn't hear me approaching the room. I opened the door slowly and there was Clyde fucking the dog shit out of another bitch in my bed. His back was turned towards me, so he didn't see me standing there with the gun pointed at them. I slammed the door behind me and he jumped from the bed like his ass was on fire. The bitch he was digging out grabbed the sheets and pulled them up to cover herself.

"Having fun?" I ask them.

"Bae! When you get back? You ain't tell me dat you was comin' home!" Clyde says as he grabs a pillow to cover himself.

"That's all that you can say? So, how long has this shit been going on? I wanna know so I can estimate how many bullets I need to put in you. I come home to surprise my man and I'm the one that ends up getting surprised. Ain't that some shit?" I say.

The girl on my bed begins to cry. "No, no, bitch! You have no fucking right to cry. You knew that you were fucking someone else's man. All these pictures around the house? The women's clothes? The feminine products in the bathroom? Bitch, miss me with that crying shit!" I yell.

"Put your clothes on and get out of here, Tasha!" Clyde tells her.

"She's not going anywhere! She goes when I tell her to go," I tell him. She starts to beg for her life, but it falls on deaf ears. "What are you covering up with a pillow for? You act like I've never seen you naked. Drop the damn pillow, Clyde!" I scream at him.

Clyde does as told and looks down at the floor in shame.

"It's big, huh? Did it feel good? Was it worth your life?" I ask her. She shakes her head and continues to beg me to let her go. Without hesitation, I shoot at her to make her shut the fuck up. I know that I'm a good shooter, but didn't think that I was THAT damn good. The bullet goes right between her eyes and she falls over dead. I look at Clyde and aim the gun at him.

"Bae, please put da gun down and we can talk 'bout dis," he tells me.

"Talk? Nigga, are you stupid? I told you that if I ever caught you fucking with another hoe, that I was going to kill you!" I scream at him. "I say what I mean and I mean what I say!" I tell him and begin to shoot at him wildly.

The rage took over me and my self-control went out the window. I kept pulling the trigger until I ran out of ammo. Luckily, Clyde had dropped to the floor and went for cover. Not one single bullet hit him and I felt some type of way about that. Suddenly, sirens could be heard approaching the house. Shit! I never thought I'd be here, stuck in Louisiana facing jail time behind some bullshit. My momma told me this place would be my downfall!

Clyde jumps up and runs towards me. I prepare to fight him, but instead of attacking me, he grabs the gun out of my hand. "Take those gloves off and hand them here," he tells me.

I give him the gloves and he puts them on.

"Pay close attention to what I tell you. Get my keys; there's a key for a safety deposit box at Regions for you. Contact Bridgette Green. She knows what to do from there. Understood?" he asks.

I nod my head, but I'm confused as to what he was doing.

"Dis is what we gone tell the police. You came home and walked in on me shooting. Dat's all you have to tell them. I'll fill in da blanks with dem. Dis whole situation is my fault, so Imma take da wrap for it," he says and kisses me before throwing on a pair of sweats and a wife beater.

After putting on some clothes and shoes, the police start to bang on the door. Clyde puts me in a chokehold and walks towards the door with the gun pointed to my head. "Step away from da door or Imma shoot dis bitch in the fuckin' head!" he shouts.

"We're moving back, put the gun down, and come out!" the officer shouts back.

"We're comin' out!" he tells them. I open the door and put my hands up while Clyde stood behind me with the gun pointed at the back of my head.

The whole situation was funny as hell. This stupid ass nigga is taking the fall for something I did after I tried to kill him. I hope he doesn't think that I'm going to hold him down after the shit I caught him doing. I played along with him and acted like the damsel in distress. "He's going to kill me! Please help me!" I screamed and ran towards the police. They rushed me into one of their cars and put me in the backseat.

"Are you okay, ma'am? Did he hurt you?" an officer asked me.

"My neck is a little sore from him choking me, but I'm okay. There's a dead girl in there!" I tell him.

"Stay here; you're safe now!" the officer tells me and closes the door.

He runs back to where all the action is and I sit back, smiling from ear to ear. Clyde surrendered to the police and they carted his dumb ass to jail. I spent about 30 minutes at the police station giving a statement. *I told them that I didn't know anything, I just walked in and heard gunshots.* I kinda respect the way Clyde's cheating ass took the fall for me. Now that he's out of my way, I can really get down to business. It's time to show Louisiana how a real boss bitch handles business.

To Be Continued...

ABOUT

TAMMY

HAWK

Tammy Hawk was born in Bossier City, Louisiana, raised in Aberdeen, Maryland and now resides in Alexandria, Louisiana with her two kids Sariah and JJ. Tammy comes from a deep rooted military family which enabled her to travel and get inspired to write.

"I will never write about places I have not been to. I put myself in my characters shoes and ask myself what would I do in their situation. I guess I have a twisted mind, which is why I'm so creative."

Tammy realized that she had a passion for writing around 11 years old. At 13 she wrote her first book which landed her in the hot seat with her mother due to it's erotic nature. She continued to let inspiration flow from a plethora of great authors such as Carl Weber, KiKi Swinson, Wahida Clark, Kwan, and Mary B. Morrison. In 2017, she decided the time is now or never to get her book published. Tammy signed with Black Authors Ink, debuting her talent with "Gotta Bmore Careful" in May, 2017. Her goal is to make writing a full time career and make it to the big screen. And with her extraordinary talent she is well on her way.

FAN PAGE

For updates on new releases follow
Tammy on her fan pages at

Facebook: https://www.facebook.com/
TammyHawkFanPage/

Twiter: https://twitter.com/TammyHawkFans

Instagram: https://www.instagram.com/
tammy20304/

#supportblackauthors

Black Authors Ink Urban Books